Diablo – The Test of Courage

Gabi Adam

Diablo –
The Test of Courage

Copyright: © Gabi Adam 2005
The plot and the names of the characters are entirely fictional.
Original Title: Die Mutprobe
Cover photo: © Bob Langrish
Cover layout: Stabenfeldt A/S
Translated by Barclay House Publishing
Typeset by Roberta L. Melzl
Editor: Bobbie Chase
Printed in Germany, 2007

ISBN: 1-933343-69-9

Stabenfeldt, Inc.
457 North Main Street
Danbury, CT 06811
www.pony.us

*For all those who don't mishandle their horses by
forcing them to perform so-called "tests of courage."*

Chapter 1

It was the second of January, and the beginning of what promised to be a very interesting year for Ricki Sulai and her friends.

"People, I'm so excited I can't even think straight, and it's freezing cold out there, too," fourteen-year-old Ricki exclaimed as she hopped from one foot to the other, trying to stay warm in the bitter cold. She'd been staring at the driveway for half an hour so as not to miss Carlotta Mancini's arrival. The former circus equestrienne star and owner of Mercy Ranch for Horses had offered to transport the already-packed luggage for Ricki and her friends Lillian Bates, Cathy Sutherland, and Kevin Thomas. The four friends were going to spend one week of the winter vacation at their elderly friend's newly opened ranch.

"I think it's so great that she's started Mercy Ranch," commented Cathy, whose foster horse, Rashid, actually belonged to Carlotta. Rashid, just like Lillian's Doc Holliday and Kevin's Sharazan, was boarded at the Sulais' stable so that the girl could ride him regularly. The stable was also home to Ricki's black gelding Diablo, and Chico, the Bates's family donkey. Chico shared his large stall with the pony mare Salena, whom Carlotta had adopted not long ago, after the owner, widower Hiram Parker, died. It was Parker who had bequeathed his property to Carlotta, making it possible for her to fulfill her dream of starting a kind of retirement home for aging and ailing horses.

There were already nine animals in residence at the ranch, animals that no longer had to worry about their futures. With Carlotta's care and attention, and the help of some local volunteer stable hands who came to the ranch every day, the horses were thriving.

"Carlotta is really a genius!" Kevin joined in, and put his arm around his girlfriend, Ricki. "It's a great idea of hers to offer riding vacations for kids in order to help finance the ranch. Really smart!"

"I think it's even better that we'll be living at the ranch during the vacation with our horses, and helping Carlotta out," laughed Lillian. "I don't think we'll have to worry about our vacations being boring ever again."

"I'm really curious to see what kind of people show up at the ranch tomorrow. I hope they're nice," said Kevin. "People who ride are always nice. Well, almost always, anyway. Hey, Ricki, know what else I find really cool?"

"No, but I think you're going to tell me, aren't you?"

"Well, I'm really excited about the party we're going to be giving on the last day at the ranch. That was a great idea of Carlotta's, and it's definitely going to be awesome!"

"Well, it is a little strange to have a party with kids you don't know. But you're probably only thinking about how many pieces of cake you're going to eat, and what kind of snacks there'll be. You probably won't care who's sitting next to you," joked Lillian, and she ducked as Kevin bent down to his grooming kit and immediately shot off a rubber band at her.

"I can tell by your reaction that I'm right," grinned Lillian before she suddenly pointed in the distance. "Hey, that looks like our luggage taxi. Do you think we forgot anything?"

"Even if we did," responded Ricki, "Mercy Ranch isn't that far away that we can't ride back over here to get something."

"That's true."

The four friends watched closely as Carlotta approached. As always, they were amused by her unique driving style.

"I'm almost sure she was a race car driver in a previous life," laughed Cathy.

And indeed, Carlotta roared into the driveway and brought her car to a sudden lurching stop. She was already waving merrily to the kids as she opened the car door.

"So, my dears, have you gotten yourselves intellectually and emotionally prepared for a hard week? We're getting a shipment of hay. That is, if the hay wagon doesn't get stuck in this deep snow. I also called the blacksmith and, of course, our guests will need to be entertained! Do you still want to come?" she asked as she got out of the car awkwardly and adjusted her crutches. Carlotta had had a riding accident years ago, and the crutches were now a part of her daily life.

"You can't scare us, Carlotta! The kids that are arriving at the ranch tomorrow can't be any harder to handle than Ricki," protested Cathy, and she hid behind her foster horse's owner.

"Just wait, Cathy, you'll be sorry!" Ricki threatened playfully with her finger before she grabbed her bag.

"Carlotta, where should I put this stuff? In the trunk or on the back seat?"

The older woman looked at the luggage in amazement. "Are you kids planning on spending the rest of your lives at my house? What did you pack?"

"Oh, Carlotta, you know how women are," Kevin winked at her.

"Indeed I do. The various necessities of young women take up a lot of room. Well, okay. Let's go!" Carlotta hobbled around her car and opened the trunk so that the friends could stow their bags.

"When are you going to start to ride over?" she wanted to know before she went in to have a cup of coffee with Ricki's mother, Brigitte.

"Right away. We're going to saddle the horses and then we're off," answered Lillian. "I think we'll need about an hour and a half to get to your ranch."

"At least," interrupted Cathy. "After all, we'll have to ride slowly. The roads are pretty icy."

"That's true!"

"Okay, kids, dress warmly. An hour and a half is a long time if you're sitting in a saddle and freezing the whole time."

"I'm sure we'll be warm enough. If necessary, we'll gallop a while in the woods." Ricki was looking forward to the cozy warmth of Carlotta's big kitchen, which was provided by a huge tiled fireplace. The girl was sure that she would have to fight for her favorite spot on the bench along the hearth wall all week long.

*

"Oh, man, I think my backside is frozen to the saddle," shivered Cathy. She held the reins in one hand while she moved the stiff fingers of the other hand.

"Gloves just aren't what they used to be," sympathized Ricki. They had just ridden past Echo Lake, which was frozen solid, and now that they had taken the direct route to Carlotta's ranch Ricki realized with a start that they still had about a half hour more to go before they reached the ranch.

The friends were frozen through and through, in spite of their thermal jackets, and to make matters worse it had begun to snow, transforming jet-black Diablo into a dappled-white horse.

Meanwhile the snow crystals had already formed little ice clumps in the horses' manes, and their moist breaths made their beards freeze.

"I think we're going to have to warm up our sweethearts first," Cathy added as she drew her head down even lower into the turned-up collar of her jacket so that her mouth was covered.

The four became increasingly quiet as the hooves of their horses sank deeper and deeper into the snow.

"I'll be glad when we get there," mumbled Ricki into her thick scarf.

When Kevin, a little while later, yelled, "I can see land!" the three girls sighed with relief.

"You know I really love to ride, but today you couldn't pay me to go any farther than Carlotta's. I'm not setting one foot out the door tonight!" Lillian straightened her shoulders and shivered, and Cathy and Ricki nodded in agreement.

*

Finally, they were there. They looked like snowmen as they rode into Carlotta's yard, hardly able to move anymore. Completely stiff with cold, they slid out of their saddles and were glad when Hal, Kieran, Lena, and Bev, the volunteers at Mercy Ranch, came running toward them to take over the horses and lead them quickly into the stable.

Carlotta, who was standing in the doorway, waved wildly at the four friends. "Come on, come on! Hurry up and come inside! You're soaked to the skin! It's a pity it had to snow so hard today!" she called, ushering them inside, and then she quickly shut the door after the frozen figures.

"Wwe sstill hahave tto ttake ccare oof the hhorses," chattered Ricki, but Carlotta just shook her head no.

"Definitely not! First of all, each of you is going to take a hot shower and change your clothes. Meanwhile, I'll make you some hot cocoa. I don't want you all to catch colds! After all, you're here to help. You can get sick at home, on your own time," she joked. "Anyway, you can be sure that Kieran and his friends will take good care of your horses. They're probably rubbing their coats dry as we speak. You'll see, they'll be back to their old selves more quickly than you will. So, no objections! Get going. You know where the bathrooms are."

On the one hand, Ricki wasn't pleased that she wasn't the one taking care of Diablo, but she had to admit that Carlotta was right. Right now she was so chilled that she wouldn't have been able to undo the saddle girth, let alone unbuckle the little straps on the snaffle. She finally followed her friends, pulled off her riding boots, and took off her wet quilted jacket. There was already a huge puddle of water around Ricki's feet from the dripping wet jacket.

"I'm ssssorry, Carlotta, I'll cccclean that up in a minute," the girl said, but the Carlotta just pushed her firmly down the hallway.

"Get going, and dry off as quickly as you can. I can handle the floor mopping myself," she grinned. She collected all four jackets and hung them up near the hearth in the kitchen to dry, before she started to make the promised cocoa.

About half an hour later, the four friends sat around the kitchen table, fresh from their showers, wrapped in thick sweaters, and enjoying the steaming cocoa and home-baked crumb cake.

Happy and content, Lucky, the mixed-breed puppy that Carlotta had gotten from Ricki, sat in front of Lillian with his tail wagging and his eyes pleading for a little piece of cake.

"Oh, this is great! I feel like a new person!" exclaimed Lillian as she stretched with pleasure. "A hot shower and a cup of cocoa can do wonders! Man, Lucky," she addressed the dog, "you're competing with Kevin for the Cake Monster title. No, you can't have anymore right now!"

"I'm glad the hot showers did you all good," replied Carlotta as she added a few more logs to the fire in the fireplace. "After all, you have to be in good shape when the kids arrive tomorrow. It's going to be quite a week. We have four ten-year-olds and two twelve-year-olds, and I'm sure they'll keep us all very busy."

"Carlotta, I take my hat off to you for taking on all this work," grinned Kevin.

"Well, how else am I going to be able to finance all of this? I don't have enough money, and each guest will bring in some for the animals. And anyway, I have a lot of people helping and supporting me, and that's what I think is really great!"

"I have to say, Carlotta, you've renovated the farm beautifully," commented Cathy, who hadn't been to the ranch in a while since she'd been recovering from a fall from her horse. "I took a look at the rooms a little while ago. They're really great. The kids are going to love them!"

"Not just the kids," said Carlotta. "I enjoy them every day, when I walk through the house. Would anyone like more cocoa?"

"Of course!"

"Yes, please!"

"Gladly!"

While Carlotta filled the cups again, the door opened, and Lena rushed in with Bev in tow.

"Wow, it's really hot in here!" groaned Lena, whose glasses fogged up immediately. "I can't see anything anymore," she said as she felt her way over to the kitchen table.

"Oh, you poor blind little bat, why don't you take off your glasses," teased Bev as she took off her jacket.

"That's a good idea," said Lena, grinning, and she shook each of the kids' hands, one after another. "It's great that you could come!"

"Hi!" Ricki scrunched up her eyes a little and looked at the two girls, who were moving about in Carlotta's kitchen as though they lived there.

"Hal and Kieran will be here in a minute," added Bev, and she reached for a piece of cake. "Mmm, delicious! Carlotta's cakes are the absolute best!" she announced, and Kevin broke out laughing.

"Yeah, I know! My mother can really bake well!" he said, and he explained to the others that Carlotta had never baked a cake in her life.

"Why should I?" laughed Carlotta. "After all, bakers have to live too, and as far as your mother is concerned, Kevin, since she started cooking for me I've gained at least ten pounds. She is really something in the kitchen... and elsewhere as well, of course," she added quickly.

"Doesn't matter! The most important thing is that there's cake left over for us." Bev, who seemed to be as big a cake fanatic as Kevin, was already stuffing a second piece into her mouth.

"Hey, hey! Bev, leave some for us!" Hal and Kieran joined them.

"So, is everything okay in the stable?" Carlotta asked.

"Of course! All of the horses have been taken care of, dried and ironed," joked Hal as he saluted merrily.

"We gave each one some hay. I hope that was okay," added Kieran.

"Of course, boys." Carlotta nodded. "You're doing a great job. Now sit down and eat. After all your work today, you earned it!"

She explained to Ricki and her friends that the two guys had already helped her that morning, setting up the rooms for the guests, and then later giving her a helping hand at the stable as well.

"Wow, I think that's wonderful," commented Cathy, admiringly.

"Well, the rooms were an exception. Usually, that's more of a girl thing," Hal defended his masculine image.

"Don't tell me you're another one of those men who

want to tie their women to the stove?" asked Lillian, amused, but Hal pretended not to hear her question.

"Who does the fantastic black gelding belong to?" asked Lena, and her eyes began to glow. "I just rubbed him dry, and he is an absolute dream horse! Is there any way that I could get to ride him?"

Kevin shook his head. "Forget about it! Ricki very seldom lets anyone ride her golden boy. She's funny that way."

"How much longer are you going to keep answering for me?" asked Ricki, laughing, and she winked at her boyfriend.

"Forever! Let's do that from now on, just like they did in the Middle Ages. The man is the woman's mouthpiece!" responded Kevin, whereby Ricki stared at him incredulously.

"Hey, are you crazy? Haven't you figured out yet that your macho-man act doesn't work with me?"

Carlotta laughed. "Well, if you're done eating, then let's sit down together and work out what we're going to do for the next eight days."

When Ricki saw that the others were still sitting in front of full plates, she got up. "I'll be right back. I just want to check on Diablo," she said, and grabbed her jacket, which had completely dried.

"I'll go with you," said Lillian spontaneously.

When the two of them had left the kitchen, Lena, with a tone of irritation in her voice, asked, "Does she think I didn't take care of her horse properly?" Carlotta just waved her anger aside.

"No, Lena, that doesn't have anything to do with it. It's just that Ricki has already experienced so much with

14

Diablo that she has to convince herself that he's all right. And that, my dear Lena, is the basic principle that should guide every horse owner," she explained to her young volunteer, who could understand the idea, but still felt a little bit insulted.

Ricki can't be much older than I am, she thought. *What has she experienced that was so great? I'll have to ask Lillian some time. Of the four of them, I like her the best!*

*

The two girlfriends had slipped quickly through the connecting door between the stable and the house.

"In this weather, this is really practical," realized Ricki as she gazed about.

Carlotta had done a truly terrific job on the stalls.

In each roomy stall there was a large window, nothing like the old dismal stalls. A wide corridor enabled the horses to be groomed and cleaned easily and efficiently, even when they were tied up next to each other, and there was a small tack room and a feed-storage area. In short, it was a pleasant, inviting stable.

All told, there were fifteen stalls, of which nine were in use.

In them stood Jonah, Hadrian, and Cora, all of whom Carlotta had saved from being killed, and all of whom were already between twenty and twenty-five years old. Sheila, a beautiful ten-year-old Black Forest mare, had also been on a list to be killed when Carlotta discovered and rescued her.

Silver, Titan, and Arabella all had problems with their joints and had been given away by their owners, since they could no longer be in shows. Corky and Jam, the two ponies, were here because their owner had moved out of the country. The owner had known Carlotta personally, and because she really cared about the ponies and wanted them to be in good hands, she'd asked the former circus performer to take them in. Corky and Jam were the only animals for whom a check arrived each month, to cover the cost of their care, and this pleased Carlotta greatly. It was very expensive to run a farm like this: insurance costs, blacksmith and vet fees, feed costs... Carlotta was grateful for every cent that was paid to help the project.

Diablo, Doc Holliday, Sharazan, and Rashid were now standing in the stalls across from the other ranch horses, and they were contentedly eating the hay that Kieran and Hal had put in their racks.

"Hi, sweetie, how are you? Do you like it here? You've got a really nice stall!" Ricki greeted her Diablo and rubbed his forehead while Lillian stroked Holli.

"Hey, the four of them really did a good job," Lillian said as she stood next to Ricki again. "You can hardly tell that the horses were ever soaking wet."

"True," agreed Ricki. "They must have brushed their coats forever. I think they're really nice kids. Strange that we never saw them on the ranch before when we visited Carlotta."

"We must have just missed them. Maybe they had already left, or hadn't arrived yet," responded Lillian, before the two girls went across the corridor to the ranch horses.

"Wow, they are really doing well." Ricki was really pleased. She talked affectionately to each of the animals. "Do you realize how good you have it here with Carlotta? And do you know that she moved here just for you? Oh, it doesn't matter; it probably doesn't really interest you. The important thing is that you have a roof over your heads and enough to eat, isn't it?"

"Don't tell them that," laughed Lillian. "I'm positive that they all know exactly who's responsible for their well-being."

"Yeah, I think so too. After all, horses can sense who likes them and who doesn't. You know, I think we'd better go back into the house," said Ricki, after glancing at her watch. They were in the stalls a lot longer than they had planned, but as always, when the girls were with their horses, they completely forgot about the time.

"I want to see Cheryl when she comes."

"Yeah, me too. She's been totally happy, ever since she got Sheila to ride and take care of."

"Happy? She's delirious!" laughed Ricki. "She doesn't talk about anything else. But why should she be any different from the rest of us?"

The two of them hurried out of the stable and went inside to join Carlotta, who was in the living room with the others.

Cheryl jumped up happily when the two girls came in.

"Hey, how long have you been here? I'm so glad to see you!" called Lillian, and she threw her arms around her friend.

"I just got here."

"It's so nice to see you all here again," interrupted Carlotta, smiling. "And, Ricki, is everything okay?"

"Yeah, of course! Thanks a lot, Lena, Diablo looks like new!" Ricki's words came straight from her heart and made the girl with the glasses feel much better.

"Don't mention it! I was glad to do it."

"Terrific. So, if everything is all set, then maybe we can

17

begin." Carlotta leaned back in her armchair and gazed at her troop of young volunteers.

"First of all, I want to tell you how much I appreciate your constant support. If it weren't for you, I would have great difficulty undertaking all of this. I'm not a spring chicken anymore!" Carlotta smiled. "Tomorrow, we will be getting six guests whose parents thought it was a good idea to start the year with a little peace and quiet while their children are being taken care of here."

"Are they boys or girls?" Bev wanted to know.

"Two boys and four girls," answered Carlotta. "The two oldest are also girls."

"Cool!" responded fourteen-year-old Lena. Maybe she would develop a real friendship with one or the other of them.

"And where are they from?" asked Kieran.

"Actually, they don't live very far away. I think, if I remember correctly, the farthest one is about fifty miles from here."

"Oh, only that far away? If I were away on vacation I'd want to be farther," commented Hal, but Bev just laughed out loud.

"For them, the most important thing is probably that they'll be away from their parents for a while," Bev said. "And of course being around the horses, I hope. As far as you're concerned, Hal, you live practically around the corner, and yet you spend all of your free time here at the ranch. I don't think it's about the distance, it's about where you want to spend your time."

"That's exactly right," said Carlotta. "All six of them are crazy about horses, or at least that's what their parents said, and therefore I think this is just the perfect place for

18

them. They can spend a lot of time with the animals, help out in the stable, and if the weather is halfway decent, they can go riding, of course. Naturally, if we have snow like today for all eight days it's going to be a problem, and we'll have to think of some kind of horse-related stuff to do. Unfortunately, we don't have an indoor riding ring that we can use in bad weather."

"Well, that means, more or less, that they've booked a riding vacation," responded Kevin, but Carlotta shook her head firmly.

"No! Absolutely not! Their parents have been informed that Mercy Ranch, as the name implies, is a retirement ranch, and they also know that it is possible for their kids to ride around a little on our horses here, but not to actually have races or anything like that. That's not the purpose of staying at the ranch."

"And what would the true purpose be?" asked Ricki, curious. "I always thought you meant to have riding vacations here."

"The purpose of this ranch is to help the children form the right relationships to older animals, or any animals, and to help them develop an understanding and empathy for them. I also want them to recognize that older and fragile animals have a right to live a decent life and can't just be disposed of. The earlier a person learns these things, the more easily it becomes a part of who they are, and they will be more responsible and careful with animals as adults. That, my dears, is what I want to teach here." Carlotta paused a while before she continued.

"So it's a vacation with horses, where riding is not the focus. Of course, they should have fun here. We can plan some games, maybe organize a drawing competition with prizes, we can teach them some facts about horses, and there will be a party. Just think about it. Anything else you come up with, I'll be glad to include."

"We could bake horse treats," suggested Cathy.

"Or we could go for a walk with the horses outside," added Lena.

"We could paint signs for each of the stalls. Carlotta, do you have a few old boards lying around?" asked Kieran, who liked to sit at home with his drawing pad and create clever designs and slogans.

"There are plenty of boards lying in the barn, left over from the renovation." Carlotta was thrilled with her volunteers' ideas. "You kids are really great! I don't think any of us will have time to be bored over the next few days," she said before she got up slowly, leaning on her crutch, and grabbed her cane.

"It's time to get the stable ready. After all, it gets dark early, and I still haven't managed to get the electrician to install a light outside for the manure pile. That means we're going to have to hurry a little to get the manure out of the stalls while there's still some daylight."

The kids jumped up at once, hurried to put on warm jackets and rubber boots, and then they all ran over to the stable.

While Carlotta was busy in the hayloft with the buckets, the boys removed manure from one stall after the other and spread clean straw on the floor.

The girls, on the other hand, brought in hay and the straw, and then distributed the herbal pellets and the enriched feed among the horses.

Soon the rhythmic sweeping of two brooms could be heard as Ricki and Cathy swept the corridor clean again.

"I think I've never enjoyed sweeping out the stalls as much in my life," laughed Ricki, and winked at her girlfriend, who felt the same way.

"It's strange. It doesn't matter where you are, it's always more fun to work in someone else's house than it is your own," she said, and paused a moment in front of Rashid's stall to give the dun horse a big kiss on his soft muzzle before she went on sweeping.

"And tomorrow morning we'll brush them all until they shine." Hal stood by his favorite, Jonah, and patted the huge draft horse affectionately on his powerful neck. "You're very special," he told him. "I really love you!"

Cathy was quiet and looked at the boy dreamily.

He's special, too, she thought to herself. But she was torn from her thoughts by Ricki poking her.

"Are you daydreaming, or something? The stable won't sweep itself," she grinned as she stuck out her tongue at her friend and started sweeping again.

*

After-dinner conversation lasted longer than Carlotta had planned, because the kids overwhelmed her with questions about her years as a circus performer, and she patiently answered all of them.

"That's it!" she said finally at about 11 o'clock and sent each of her helpers, one after the other, into the bathroom to get ready for bed.

"Sleep tight, kids, and thanks again for being here," Carlotta called after them before she herself went to bed.

21

However it took her a long time to fall asleep, because, she had to admit, she was a little excited, too, thinking about the coming week. After all, it was the first time that she would be receiving guests at the ranch.

"It'll be fine," she murmured to herself, now half asleep, before finally dozing off.

Chapter 2

Ricki woke up early the next morning. One glance out of the window told her that it hadn't snowed much during the night; however, she had the impression that it had gotten much colder outside. Quietly, so as not to wake her roommates Lillian and Cathy, she got dressed and tiptoed out of the room and along the hallway to the bathroom.

Soon after she was on her way to the kitchen. Quickly she began to set the table for breakfast and soon, thanks to her efforts, the aroma of freshly brewed coffee permeated the house.

Carlotta appeared in the doorway about half an hour later. "Good morning, Ricki. Mmm, that smells so good! Don't tell me you've already made coffee? Fabulous! That's just what I need right now to wake up! Do you always get up this early?" she asked as she poured herself a cup of coffee.

"Not usually," admitted Ricki. "By the way, the others are still sleeping. Should I have woken them?"

"No, no, let them get their sleep. How was your night?"

"I dreamed something stupid, and thankfully I can't remember what it was," the girl replied and put the bread and jam on the table. "Anything missing?"

Carlotta looked at the table thoughtfully.

"Well, what you've put out is enough for me; however, your friends might like some eggs for breakfast," she said. But Ricki just shook her head.

"Carlotta, let's not even ask them, otherwise we'll be getting orders for gourmet breakfasts: pancakes and sausages, eggs Benedict... stuff like that. I know these kids and their appetites!"

Carlotta had to laugh. She was no stranger to Ricki's friends' appetites. "It's actually good that we have a few minutes alone," she said as she eased herself into a chair. "I want to talk with you about one of the girls who's arriving today."

Ricki sat down, too, with a cup of tea and milk, and looked at Carlotta in anticipation. "What's this about?"

"Well, how can I say this? One of the twelve-year-olds, her name is Caitlin Lisser, seems to be a little difficult. Her mother passed away about six months ago and, according to her father, she seems to have changed completely over the past few months. He said she used to be affectionate and cooperative, but ever since her mother's death, she's built a wall around herself and just yells at people."

"Oh, boy! This is already starting to sound so not like a totally 'relaxing' week," groaned Ricki.

"Don't complain, dear. I think we just have to feel our way – slowly and carefully – around Caitlin, so that we can help her find herself again. Her father hopes that she'll be reminded of who she was through her dealings with the

horses and her relationship with all of us. Ricki, I thought...
I mean, I want to ask you if you can pay a little extra
attention to this girl."

Ricki swallowed hard. *Terrific!* she thought. *I'm
supposed to baby-sit a bad-tempered, quarrelsome little
brat! I just hope nothing goes wrong.*

"Of course I will, if you want me to," she responded
softly and avoided looking directly at Carlotta so that the
ranch owner wouldn't be able to read her mind.

"I know how you must feel, but I think if anyone can
manage to get through to this girl, it'll be you." Carlotta
nodded at Ricki encouragingly. "You can do it, I'm sure.
But, Ricki, please, don't tell the others just yet. I don't want
them to develop negative feelings toward Caitlin right from
the start."

"Okay." Ricki took a deep breath and fixed herself a
piece of toast with jam, but her mind was on other things.

Gradually, one by one, Carlotta's volunteers came down
to breakfast, some of them still not completely awake.

"Good morning, everyone," beamed the lady of the
house, smiling at them. "I hope you all slept well. First get
some breakfast, and then we'll go over to the stalls. I think
our animals are probably hungry, too."

That worked. All of a sudden even Lena, who was still
very sleepy, woke up. If it was about horses, she forgot
everything else, even her exhaustion.

*

About half an hour later, all eight of the young people were
busy working around the stalls and the horses, making sure
that everything looked especially nice and tidy. After all,

Carlotta hoped that her young guests would get such a good impression of the place that they'd want to come back. By the time they finished, the kids realized that they could work like this all the time, with or without the added incentive of guests.

"This is the way it should be," commented Carlotta, pleased with what the kids had accomplished, and she glanced at her watch. "Eight o'clock. We're right on schedule. I expect the first ones to arrive around ten, and by lunchtime they should all be here."

"I'm so curious to see what they're like," exclaimed Bev, as Ricki gave Carlotta a sidelong glance.

"Hey, Carlotta, I just remembered. Mom said you should call her and tell her if you need anything for the kitchen. She wants to go shopping first, before she comes here to cook," called Kevin from Jam's stall.

"Well, thank heavens you told me in time," replied Carlotta. "Otherwise we would have been eating nothing but yogurt for the entire week. I'll give her a call right away. Oh, by the way, Kevin, please remember to treat Jam's hooves with that antifungal ointment every morning. It's on the shelf in the tack room."

"Okay." Kevin grinned at the pony gelding. "You could have told me that yourself, couldn't you?" he said, but Jam just kept on eating and paying him no attention, as though his hooves were of no concern to him.

*

Carlotta was right. At ten o'clock the first three cars approached.

"Thank goodness the snowplow came by already," she said as she watched the arrival of the guests from the stable.

26

"Cathy, would you please make some cocoa, and put two more logs on the fire so that it doesn't go out? Kieran and Hal, please stay nearby so that you can show the guests to their rooms and help them carry their luggage. Okay?"

"Of course!" The two boys stood next to Carlotta, ready to help, while the others quickly put the tools and grooming implements away in the tack room.

"I am so excited," said Lena to her friend Bev, and she took off her glasses for the umpteenth time to clean them.

"If you keep doing that you're not going to have any glass left in the frames," joked Lillian. "I think you're more nervous than the guests who are on their way here!"

"Does that surprise you?" complained Lena. "After all, it's the first time strangers will be vacationing at our ranch."

"Our ranch!" Kevin grinned, but he was just as on edge as the Lena. Nevertheless, he said, "I'm sure Carlotta has everything under control." He put his arm around Ricki and they both walked over to the window to see what was happening. They could tell that there were different conversations going on in the arriving vehicles.

*

"Oh, man, is that the ranch? Totally cool!" Frankie had pressed his nose flat against the car's fogged-up window.

"Cool?" questioned Mr. Simons. "You can say that again. We're only a few miles from home, and although the streets back home are already completely cleared, they're covered in snow here! Unbelievable. I'm beginning to wonder why I agreed to let you come to a horse ranch this time of year."

27

Frankie grinned. "Because you and Mom wanted to have some peace and quiet at home without me!"

Mr. Simons raised one eyebrow and glanced sideways at his son. "You make it sound as though we wanted to get rid of you. Is that the way you see it?"

Frankie shrugged his shoulders indifferently. "Whatever! The main thing is that I'll have a full week to be around horses. This is going to be the best."

"I don't think you'll be spending all your time in the stalls. After all, these animals need some peace, too, don't you think?"

Mr. Simons glanced in the rearview mirror. "I think the people behind us are driving to the ranch, too."

"Really?" Frankie's head turned around quickly, and he waved wildly to the two people in the car following them, but his wave wasn't returned.

*

Caitlin Lisser sat in the front passenger seat of her father's car with her head pulled down and just rolled her eyes when she saw Frankie waving through the quickly moving windshield wipers.

"Great! Don't tell me that little kid up there booked this stupid horse vacation too! Dad, can't you just turn around and drive back home? I don't feel like doing any of this!"

"Just wait and see. You always said you wanted to spend a few days at a ranch." Caitlin's father stared straight ahead.

"That was a long time ago. What am I supposed to do here? There's snow on the ground, it's cold, there's no indoor riding ring, just tired worn-out old horses and stupid little kids. I don't want to be here! If you don't take me back with you, I'll run away! I swear it!" Caitlin's eyes sparkled with anger.

"Caitlin, please, you weren't like this before," mumbled Mr. Lisser almost inaudibly.

"Before?" The girl laughed humorlessly and much too loudly. "Before! Before, everything was different! Turn around! I really don't feel like doing any of this stuff here. Are you listening? You don't seem to be interested in finding out what I want!"

Mr. Lisser didn't answer her.

"Thanks a lot for not caring about me! Mom would never have forced me to do anything like this."

"Caitlin, that's enough," her father said, softly but firmly.

"It's true."

"I said, that's enough. Look, we're almost there."

The girl had tears of anger in her eyes. "Just great! I can't wait! Why couldn't you have left me at home? Then you could have spent a few wonderful days here yourself at the end of the world, if you can't stand me anymore."

Caitlin's father decided not to answer his daughter's angry, hate-filled questions. He hoped that the distractions of the ranch – working with the horses and making new friends – would help her get back to normal soon. In spite of everything, he was sure that she knew how much he loved her.

*

"Mom, please tell Michelle that she can't keep telling me what to do!" Amy Kress shouted right into her mother's ear as her older sister grinned annoyingly.

"If you bother me as much at the ranch as you do at home, then you're in trouble. You always act like such an idiot!"

"I'm not an idiot! You're an idiot! Mom, please tell her that I'm not an idiot! That's really mean."

Mrs. Kress rolled her eyes angrily. "I'm beginning to think that I made a mistake registering both of you here together!"

Michelle nodded in agreement. "That's great, but you figured it out a little too late, Mom! Couldn't you just take that little brat back home with you and leave me here by myself?"

Amy howled. "No! I want to stay here with the horses. Why don't you go back home, if you're so unhappy?"

"Simple, dummy. Who brought home the address of Mercy Ranch, me or you?"

"I'm not a dummy!"

"Of course you're a dummy!"

"Michelle, I want you to stop now, too, okay? No normal person could stand your constant bickering!"

The older girl nodded approval at her mother. "Exactly! You don't want to do this to the people at the ranch, do you?"

"I'm ashamed when I imagine all the rude things you two will say to each other! People will think I haven't taught you girls any manners at all!"

"Ha, ha, Mom, then you must have done something wrong, didn't you?" Michelle stretched and pinched her sister's upper arm.

"Ouch! Are you crazy?"

"Amy, please, stop being such a pest!"

"But Michelle pinched –"

"I didn't do anything!"

Mrs. Kress slowed the car, and when it had finally come to a stop at the side of the road, she turned her head toward her two daughters. "Now I want you two to listen carefully. There are two possibilities! Either you two are going to behave and treat each other with respect, or we're going to turn around right now and neither one of you is going to go stay at Mercy Ranch!"

Michelle made a face. "You can't do that! I paid for half of this vacation myself!"

"I don't care!"

"Na, na, nanana, I didn't have to pay anything!" Amy stuck her tongue out at her older sister.

"How nice for you! Just leave me alone! I don't feel like missing out on the horses just because of you!"

"What do you mean, because of me?"

"Because you're such an idiot!"

"I'm not an idiot!"

"Apparently you two didn't understand me!" Mrs. Kress announced, her eyes sparkling threateningly.

Michelle looked back at her mother and then she sat back in her seat and pouted. Amy sensed, too, that she would have to be careful.

"Finally! See! You can behave, when the motivation is strong enough." Mrs. Kress turned back to the road, put the car in gear, and slowly drove the last few yards to the ranch.

*

A short while later, the last two guests arrived, and while Carlotta sat with the parents and drank coffee in the living room, Cheryl and Bev took the twins, Karen and Patrick, through the house to show them their rooms.

"Your roommates are already here. You'll be sleeping in rooms with three beds each." Cheryl knocked on one of the doors, and they immediately heard loud laughter coming from within.

31

"This is Patrick and Karen," Bev introduced the two, and Kevin got up immediately.

"Hey, Patrick! It's great that you're here! Come right in! This is Frankie and I'm Kevin. Hey, Karen, you'll be sleeping with Amy and Lillian, one door farther down."

"Okay." Karen looked a little strangely at Frankie, who was still lying on the floor and trying, unsuccessfully, to stop his laughing fit.

"Men! Or at least guys who are supposed to become men!" said Cheryl. She grinned and took the girl's arm and propelled her next door where Karen was heartily greeted by her roommates. Soon there was a happy and relaxed atmosphere in this room as well. Only in the room across the hall was the atmosphere frosty, although Ricki tried hard to convince Michelle and Caitlin that a three-bed room had its advantages.

"This is just terrific!" commented Caitlin sarcastically, and remained standing there with her bag under her arm. "I didn't want to come here in the first place. So what makes you think I want to be together with you at night, too? If I don't get a single room, I'm leaving!"

Michelle and Ricki looked at each other in amazement.

"Well, I think it's fabulous! We can talk all night, and –" Michelle started.

"Well, have fun... and good-bye!" Caitlin turned on her heel and ran straight downstairs and right into Carlotta.

"Caitlin, where are you going?" Carlotta asked pleasantly.

"Where is my father? I'm going to go back home with him!" The girl tried to squeeze past her but Carlotta's cane was in her way.

"Why? Don't you like it here?"

"No!"

"Oh!" Carlotta didn't say anything further, but just stared hard at Caitlin.

After a while, Caitlin began to feel unsure of herself under Carlotta's scrutiny.

"Would you please... would you please let me get past you?" the girl asked timidly.

"Of course! You aren't a prisoner here." Carlotta took a step to the side so that Caitlin could just squeeze past her in the narrow hallway.

The girl kept going, slowly, and felt Carlotta's penetrating stare on the back of her neck. It was a feeling that made her uncomfortable.

Caitlin swallowed, then she stopped and turned around slowly.

"Don't you want to know why I want to go back home?" she asked abruptly, but Carlotta just shrugged her shoulders.

"You already said you don't like it here."

"Hmm..."

"Or is there perhaps a completely different reason?" Carlotta asked again, a few seconds later, but Caitlin couldn't answer her. Something forced her to keep her mouth closed and not say anything.

"Come with me," said Carlotta, and hobbled over to the girl and grasped her around the shoulder. She pushed her along gently, and then asked her to put her bag down, and left the house with her. Right afterward they entered the stalls.

"I thought you should at least see the horses before you leave," said Carlotta, gazing affectionately at the animals, who greeted her contentedly.

Caitlin took a deep breath. She loved horses more than anything, and now, seeing all the horses looking at her full of curiosity, her heart gave a leap. How long had she been waiting to get a whiff of a stable again? How long had she been longing to touch the warm coat of a horse and to feel its strength and at the same time its gentleness?

As if in a trance, Caitlin moved toward the first stall, where Hadrian was waiting impatiently for a treat and scratching the ground with his front hoof.

"That's one of our seniors who was almost put down, but now, thank goodness, he can live out his life without fear. Next to him is Arabella, then Jonah, Sheila, Cora... " Carlotta told her a little bit about each horse, and when she was almost finished with her tour of the stable, Caitlin stood in front of Diablo with shining eyes, and he looked back at her, his eyes huge.

"These four stable companions," Carlotta explained, pointing at Diablo, Rashid, Sharazan, and Doc Holliday, "are guests here at the ranch. Normally, they're in another stable. This one here," Carlotta nodded at the black horse, "belongs to Ricki, your roommate. His name is Diablo."

Caitlin whistled softly.

"Wow, he belongs to Ricki?" she asked incredulously. Then, after a long pause, she asked quietly, more to herself than to her host, "When you own a horse like this, you must be the happiest person in the world, don't you think?"

"Well, I think that everyone who owns a horse is happy, whether it's a wonderful gelding like Diablo or a shaggy little pony. There are people who are happy to own a guinea pig. I think that every animal has the ability to make its person feel happy."

Caitlin was still staring at the black horse. "But something like him... he's really special."

Carlotta laid her hand on the girl's shoulder. "Each one of the animals here is special. Just like every human being is special. You too!" She sensed that Caitlin stiffened at her words.

"Look here, most of these animals have experienced terrible things, frightening situations, torture, and beatings. Here they have to learn to trust in themselves again and also to trust other people again. That's not easy sometimes. But if we remind ourselves how we have felt in specific situations, then it's easier to put ourselves in their places and help them to become themselves again. Wouldn't you like to help us with this wonderful task, Caitlin?"

The girl pressed her lips together before she began to shake her head slowly.

"Why not?"

Caitlin swallowed hard. "Because... because I... because..."

Carlotta put her hand underneath the girl's chin, and lifted her face gently so that she could look her in the eyes. "We don't just help the animals, Caitlin. It works both ways." She paused a moment before she continued. "Look, I know how you feel, even though I didn't lose my mother at your age. However, my daughter died very young, and I know all too well what losing a loved one means. Back then I had shut myself off from the rest of the world. I didn't want to hear anything or see anything. But even the greatest loneliness didn't bring my daughter back to me. So I turned more and more to animals, who finally enabled me to open up to other people again."

Caitlin seemed to look straight through Carlotta. She

heard her words and understood what they meant, but she wasn't sure if she even wanted others to help her, animals or people. She just wanted to be left alone.

Mommy! Something screamed inside the girl. *Mommy, why did you leave me here alone? My life was so wonderful until you left! Now nothing is the way it was! Nothing! And now I'm here at this horse ranch in the middle of nowhere and I'm supposed to act as if everything is just fine. I just can't! I want to go home, but Dad can't stand me anymore either. Mommy, why not?*

Tears ran out of Caitlin's vacant eyes just as her father's voice called from the entrance to the stable.

"Caitlin?! Oh, here you are. I'm leaving now."

The girl didn't react to his words.

Carlotta kept looking at her before she said to her, quietly, "Caitlin, of course you can decide to leave now with your father, but it would be nice if you would give the horses – and these great kids – a chance to help you. I'm sure that these eight days would be good for you if you spent them here."

"What –?" began Mr. Lisser, but Carlotta silenced him with one gesture of her hand.

"Okay," Caitlin whispered almost inaudibly. She sniffed loudly, wiped her eyes with the back of her hand, and almost fell over forward when Diablo pushed against her back with his head.

A small smile lit up her face as she looked up at the enormous black horse before she turned to her father. "Then I'll see you in a week, Dad," she said finally, and then she ran over to him and wrapped her arms around his neck.

"Caitlin? Is everything all right with you?" Bewildered, he stroked her hair and looked at Carlotta, undecided, as she came hobbling over to him.

"Don't worry, Mr. Lisser," she said with a loving glance at the girl. "I think it's been a long time since things were as okay as they are now!" Neither of the two adults, however, could imagine what Caitlin was really thinking.

Chapter 3

The whole group ran laughing into Carlotta's kitchen, where Caroline Thomas, Kevin's mother, had prepared a huge pot of hearty beef stew and had already extended the table and set it beautifully.

"Well, are you all hungry?" she asked merrily, and greeted them with a wave of her cooking spoon.

"Of course! Always!" answered Kevin loudly.

"I hope you like stew. I'm a little late with lunch," she apologized, but Ricki just waved her apologies aside.

"Stew is wonderful! It's perfect for cold weather like this. Let's go, people, sit down. Where's Carlotta?"

"I was wondering that myself. Maybe she's in the stable? Maybe we should wait –?" Kieran hadn't even finished his sentence when the owner of Mercy Ranch came into the room, leading a reluctant Caitlin behind her.

"Oh, did you change your mind after all?" Michelle blurted out without thinking before Ricki could stop her.

Immediately, Caitlin's face turned to stone and she stood

still. "I can leave if you don't want me here!" she snapped back, as Carlotta and Ricki quickly exchanged glances.

"Hey, Caitlin, Michelle didn't mean it like that. I think it's great that you're staying. You'll see. You won't regret it!" Ricki walked over to the girl and put out her hand to take her bag. "Come on, sit down with the others, and I'll take your bag upstairs. And by the way, you'll be glad to hear, I don't snore."

Caitlin pushed Ricki's hand away. "Keep your hands off my bag. I don't need your help. There's nothing wrong with my legs. I can take it upstairs myself!"

Ricki was angered by the rude manner in which her offer of help had been rebuffed, but then she remembered what Carlotta had told her about this girl so she kept smiling but took a step back. "As you like. But hurry, or the stew will get cold."

Caitlin made a face. "I don't like stew anyway!"

"Oh, I'm really sorry!" Kevin's mother wiped her hands on her apron.

"You don't have to be sorry. I'm not going to be staying long anyway!" With these words the twelve-year-old disappeared in the direction of the bedrooms.

"Wow, what a scene!" Cathy stood at the table, and as Kevin's mother filled the plates she passed them around to the guests. "What's wrong with her? She acts like a princess!"

Amy and Karen whispered something to each other that no one else overheard, and then they giggled and bent over their plates.

Frankie and Patrick, however, agreed that only girls could be that weird, and Kieran made a pretty harsh comment back at them, but Carlotta stopped them all decisively.

39

"So, my dears, now that you've all done enough talking about her, I want to ask you, please, to treat everyone with respect," she said, and she gave each one a piercing glance.

"Of course, Carlotta. No problem," responded Hal. "Maybe you should tell Caitlin that too!"

"Let me worry about her, okay?"

"Umm, maybe she's just not in a good mood today," suggested Ricki, who remembered that she was supposed to keep quiet about Caitlin's situation for a while. "After all, we all have bad days once in a while."

"Well, then I hope this is her one and only bad day. If she's going to act like this everyday it's going to be an ugly eight-day vacation," responded Lena with her mouth full of food. "Oh, Mrs. Thomas, your stew is really fantastic. Delicious!" Lena smiled broadly at Kevin's mother as she downed another spoonful.

Hearing the noise she was making, Bev rolled her eyes. "Gee, Lena, hasn't anyone ever shown you how to eat with a knife and fork?"

"Why? Since when do you eat stew with a knife and fork?"

"I meant your slurping!"

"Ugh, that's disgusting!" Caitlin had come back into the kitchen and now she was staring, repulsed, at the girl with the glasses.

"Come in and sit down with us," Carlotta invited the girl, ignoring Caitlin's objections. "When we've all finished eating we'll wash the dishes together, and then we'll take a tour through the stable so you can get acquainted with the animals. Come on, Caitlin, grab your plate. At Mercy Ranch we live together, work together, and eat together! Unfortunately, this isn't a hotel, so I can't offer you a choice of menu, but if I know the culinary talents of Kevin's mother, she won't put anything in front of us we can't eat!" Carlotta laughed but her voice didn't allow any talking back.

Sighing, Caitlin submitted to her fate, probably because everyone was looking at her, waiting for her to eat at least one spoonful.

"I don't like this stuff," she grumbled quietly to herself, although she had to admit that she had never tasted such a delicious stew before.

"See, it's not that bad!" Cheryl winked at Lillian, who shook her head slightly.

"Very good! The eating problem is solved for now," commented Carlotta, laughing. "Later, when we're back inside, we'll get together and work out a plan for who helps whom with what. We have enough work here, so it won't get boring for any of you. Two of you will help with breakfast, two for lunch, and two for dinner, and then there's dishwashing, grooming the horses, and working in the stable. Of course, the plan will be changed each day, and you can decide now, with whom you want to do what."

"And when can we go riding?" asked Michelle with shining eyes.

Carlotta smiled at her. "Don't worry, I don't have to divide you up for riding. There are enough horses here who need exercise, and if the weather allows you'll be getting up into the saddle every day!"

"Oh, great!" Amy clapped her hands in anticipation, and Frankie got hiccups from the excitement.

"That... *hick*... is really great... *hick*!" he managed to say with some difficulty, which got everyone laughing with him.

41

"Hey, kid, you have to learn how to eat and speak clearly before you start thinking about getting on a horse," laughed Kieran, and suddenly he went into a coughing fit because he had swallowed a pea that got caught in his windpipe.

"*Hah,* he should talk!" Bev giggled, and she pushed her empty plate away from her. "Oh, I am so full! How am I going to be able to work after this?"

"Chow hound!" Hal gave her a poke in the ribs. "How much did you eat? You know, for each pea, you have to clean out one stall!"

Bev groaned. "This is going to be the end of me. I'll have to keep forking out the manure from the stalls for the rest of my life!"

"Oh, she's always exaggerating!"

They continued to joke around like that for quite a while, and pretty soon the newcomers had gotten comfortable enough to joke with them.

"The people here are really nice!" whispered Patrick to Frankie, who nodded in agreement. "It's going to be really great here!"

"Nope, it's already great!" contradicted the boy, and then he got up voluntarily to collect the empty dishes from the table. His mother would have been very pleased with him, or maybe she would have thought that her son was sick, because at home Frankie left everything lying where it was.

Almost as though on command, the others pushed their chairs back in order to help.

Caroline Thomas put her hands on her hips, laughed, and winked at her son.

"You could learn a lot from them, my son," she commented

happily before returning to the sink to wash the dishes. Carlotta was already distributing the dishtowels.

"No way," groaned Kevin. "I bet none of these kids is this helpful in their own house."

"What? Of course!" replied one kid in mock shock.

"At my house?"

"Always!" someone said, completely unconvincingly. Grinning, Kevin grabbed a wet sponge and began to wipe off the table. "You liars!"

*

In less than fifteen minutes the kitchen was spotlessly clean, and Carlotta nodded approvingly. "As the saying goes, many hands make light work! See, no one had to do too much work, and now we have a lot of time for other things." She scanned the expectant faces quickly. "Well, let's go to the stable. I know you can hardly wait."

"Finally!" whispered Frankie to Patrick, and he gave him a poke in the side.

"Stop it, Frankie. I bet I already have a zillion bruises! At the end of the week, Mom's going to ask me who was beating me up."

"Sure, and you're probably going to blame me as usual," grumbled Karen.

"Naturally!" grinned her brother. "And then you'll get at least two days of no television!"

"No kidding! Siblings are the worst!" Michelle gave her sister Amy a knowing look.

"Exactly," Amy responded and was about to say something equally mean, but Carlotta held up her hands for them to stop.

43

"So, enough family fun. If you want to fight, do it at home, but not here. Follow me!"

"Carlotta has spoken!" whispered Ricki, and she took Caitlin's arm almost automatically, since she was standing next to her. "Come on, let's go. You'll see, you'll like the horses!"

Caitlin had become as stiff as a board and looked Ricki up and down. "Would you mind letting go of me? I can't stand people touching me!"

"Oh, sorry, it won't happen again." Ricki took a step back immediately. "I didn't mean to get too close!"

"But you did!"

"Don't make such a big deal out of it, Caitlin. Ricki was just trying to be nice!" commented Kieran, who was right behind the two girls.

"No one needs to be nice to me!" responded the twelve-year-old aggressively, with arched eyebrows.

"Considering how nasty you're acting, I doubt that anyone would want to take the chance of being nice to you. Come on, Ricki!"

Kieran wanted to pull Diablo's owner with him, but she shook her head very slightly, and so the boy let go of her hand and left her there as he hurried after the others, who had already left the kitchen.

Kevin's mother had left the kitchen as well, and so the two girls were alone in the empty room.

Ricki struggled with herself about what to say. On the one hand, she was furious that Caitlin seemed to have a problem with everything and everybody. On the other hand, she tried to put herself in the twelve-year-old's shoes. It must be incredibly difficult to grow up without a mother, and Ricki could understand why Caitlin had built such a high wall around herself. It was clear that she didn't want people to get near her real feelings.

"Hey, I really didn't mean –" she began, but Caitlin's snappish "Forget it!" interrupted her before she could even finish her sentence. Astonished, Ricki watched as Caitlin ran out of the kitchen, as though wolves were after her, and thundered up the stairs, where she slammed the door to the bedroom shut.

Puzzled and discouraged, Ricki shrugged her shoulders and then slowly started walking to catch up with the others.

What can I do? she asked herself. She dragged her feet across the hallway and was just about to open the connecting door to the stable when she heard muted sobbing coming from the second floor.

Caitlin!

"Darn it!" Ricki struggled with herself and stared at her hand, which was still on the doorknob. Should she go back? Should she try to talk to Caitlin, or would it be better just to let her have a good cry in private?

So many thoughts went through Ricki's head, and she was tempted to join the others in the stable. Their companionship and that of the horses would have appealed to her much more than what was probably awaiting her if she went up to Caitlin's room. But then, in her mind's eye, Ricki saw the image of Carlotta before her, and she remembered her promise that she would look after Caitlin.

"If I had known how difficult she was going to be, I wouldn't have been so quick to give Carlotta my word," sighed Ricki deeply, but then she turned and slowly climbed the stairs.

*

"Oh, he's so cute!" Amy was standing in front of Jam and couldn't tear her eyes away from the pony. "Did you save him too?" She looked up at Carlotta.

"No, he and Corky, the one next to him, belong to a friend who's living overseas right now."

"Then we probably won't be allowed to ride Jam, will we?" Amy's face reflected her disappointment, but when Carlotta smiled at her and said, "Yes, you can," the girl's heart jumped for joy.

"If you want, you can take him as your horse to care for during the week. And as far as riding goes, I don't think his owner would have anything against him getting some exercise now and then."

Now Amy was beside herself with joy. She hugged Jam's strong neck with all her might, and pressed her face into his coat, while Jam snorted and sniffed all over her sweater contentedly.

"It seems as if your friendship is sealed," laughed Carlotta, and she turned to her other guests.

"And the rest of you?" she asked, curious. "Have you found your favorites yet?"

"Oh, yeah!" Michelle pointed to old Hadrian. "If it's all right with you, I'd like to take this one here. He looks so sweet!"

"Hadrian doesn't just look sweet, he is sweet. That's true of all of the other horses as well. Not one of them kicks or bites or is mean in any way. Good, Michelle, then you'll take care of Hadrian."

"I'd like to take care of Silver," Frankie spoke up.

"And I'd like Titan!" said Patrick as he stroked the horse's forehead tenderly.

"What? Titan? I thought you wanted Corky." Karen looked at her brother in amazement.

"I just changed my mind."

"That's great! What luck! Carlotta, can I have Corky, then?"

"Of course. So, have you all found an animal you like?"

"Miss hissy-fit Lisser is still missing! But she's probably pouting in the corner somewhere," said Kieran, and bit his lip as he saw Carlotta's look of disappointment and reproach.

"Caitlin saw the horses a while ago. I'll ask her later which animal she wants to take on."

Bev and Hal looked at each other in surprise at Carlotta's words. "Why did Caitlin have a special tour of the stable?"

"It wasn't a special tour, it just turned out that way."

"Can we stay in the stable for a while, Mrs. Mancini?"

Carlotta had to laugh when she saw Amy's pleading look. "Don't worry, dear, you can stay in the stable for a long time, if you like. The blacksmith will be here in about fifteen minutes, and I would like you to take the horses out of their stalls and scrape out their hooves so that he can see what needs to be done. Make sure you get them really clean. Tie up the horses in the corridor in front of their stalls. You'll find the hoof picks in the tack room, in the appropriate grooming boxes. The names of the horses are on everything. I want to ask you to put everything back where you got it, so that no one needs to search for anything afterward. By the way, you can all call me Carlotta. When you call me Mrs. Mancini, I feel as old as my own grandmother." The owner of the ranch winked at the kids mischievously. "Where's Ricki?" she asked suddenly, and looked around.

Kevin, who was just coming out of Sharazan's stall, shrugged his shoulders. "I have no idea. She can't be far.

47

Maybe Mom's stew didn't agree with her. No, what am I saying? But what I would really like to know is where Gandalf is. Have you seen him yet today, Carlotta?"

"Yes, he was lying in front of the living room fireplace with Lucky a while ago."

Kevin exhaled in relief. "Then everything's fine. I thought maybe he'd gone on a long walk by himself." The boy remembered all too well that not very long ago he and his friends had ridden through the freezing countryside for more than two hours looking for his dog, whom Mrs. Thomas had brought with her to the ranch this morning.

Lillian bent over laughing.

"Long walk, my eye!" she explained to the kids standing around her. "Our hands were almost frozen – stuck to the reins by the time we got home again. And then realized that, unbeknownst to us, Gandalf had decided to take a nap under the bench in the kitchen. We could have spared ourselves the icy ride, but Kevin had us all upset, and he started spouting the worst possible scenarios."

"He really almost drove us crazy. He wanted to organize a search party for his dog and –" Cathy continued, but Kevin just waved her words aside.

"Don't believe anything these girls tell you," he grinned. "They always exaggerate."

"Whatever!"

"I have to go see what's happened to Ricki and Caitlin," said Carlotta, and she asked Kieran to be in charge and make sure that all the horses were tied up correctly and their hooves well cleaned. "I'll be right back," she called over her shoulder as she left the stable.

*

48

Ricki took a deep breath before she carefully turned the knob and softly entered the room where Caitlin lay sobbing on the bed, her face pressed into a pillow.

For a moment Ricki just stood there and stared at the unhappy girl in front of her.

If only it wasn't so difficult to find a beginning, she thought and struggled to find the right words that would comfort Caitlin. But she just didn't know what to say.

After a while, she cleared her throat quietly to at least show that she was there. She felt that Caitlin had a right to know that she wasn't alone in the room.

The girl was startled and sat up, and when she recognized Ricki through her tears, Caitlin's face turned bright red.

"And?" she yelled. "Do you enjoy watching someone cry? What are you doing here? Get out! I want to be alone!"

"I'm sorry. I didn't know that you –"

"You're sorry? That's swell!"

"Caitlin, can I help you in any way?"

"Yes! Just leave me alone! You don't have to play the Good Samaritan! I don't need you!"

Ricki swallowed hard, and again she regretted that she had promised Carlotta to help Caitlin.

"I'm no Good Samaritan, but I thought that maybe you might like to talk about it."

Caitlin's eyes shot daggers of hate. "Talk about it? About what? That I don't have a mother anymore, or about the weather? What do you want to know? How I feel? Like garbage! But don't worry about it. You'll forget all about me by next week, when your mother puts your dinner in front of you! Yeah, be happy that you still have your old lady!"

49

Ricki ground her teeth. "Why are you talking like this?"

"How?"

"Why did you say 'old lady'? I don't like it when someone calls my mother that."

"Then call her what you want. Just leave me alone, and then you and I won't have a problem!" Caitlin turned her face away, reached for a tissue from the box on the nightstand, blew her nose loudly, and then looked out the window purposefully, in the hope that Ricki would leave. After a while, when she didn't hear anything in the room, she turned around again, but Ricki was still standing in the same spot.

"Can't you just leave? *Please*," said Caitlin, with emphasis, but Ricki just stared at her.

"You loved her very much, didn't you?" she asked softly, but the twelve-year-old just made an ugly face.

"Loved? No, I really hated her! She was mean, and she hit me, and she was a lousy mother! Are you satisfied?"

Ricki's face looked like stone and didn't show what she was actually feeling when she heard Caitlin's rant. "Why are you saying those things? Do you think it'll make things easier to deal with?"

Caitlin sighed deeply. "What do you know? And what do you want to hear? Yeah, I had a wonderful mother. Are you satisfied now?"

"No!"

Caitlin's gaze wandered restlessly across the room before it returned to remain fixed on Ricki's eyes.

"You will never understand how I feel! No one will! At least no one who hasn't experienced what I have." She paused, and Ricki tried hard not to make a sound.

50

"Have you ever experienced what it's like when a person dies? I mean, how a person dies a little more each day? Really slowly? Bit by bit? When you see how a person who is incredibly important to you becomes less and less each day... when her face hollows out... when she loses her hair? You have no idea what it's like to experience that... for weeks and months..." Caitlin's voice got quieter and quieter, and it seemed as if she was almost in a trance, speaking in monotone, without any emotion, as though someone else were speaking for her.

Ricki hardly dared to breathe, but she felt her heart beating almost up to her throat.

Oh no, she thought. *She's not talking about some film, or some novel, she's talking about her mother! When I try to imagine that... Oh, please, not that! You always think something like that can never happen to you, and yet here's a girl describing the death of her mother!*

"She was a wonderful person, but she left me alone! Dad and me! Why did she do that? Why? It's not fair! I mean, why did she just die? That was mean of her! So cruel!" Caitlin came out of her stiffness and stared at Ricki with a desperate rage. She hardly noticed that endless tears flowed down her cheeks.

Ricki felt like she could feel the girl's pain and would have liked to cry with her, but she knew that wouldn't help Caitlin.

Slowly, she took a step toward her and put her hand hesitantly on Caitlin's shoulder. "Caitlin... I am so sorry!" she said softly. "I know how you feel."

"You don't know anything! You can't know!"

Ricki nodded. "You're right. I can't know, but I can imagine –"

51

"You can't even imagine! No one can if they haven't experienced it themselves!"

Ricki's brain was whirling. She had no idea what she could say to Caitlin in order to comfort her.

"Okay," she began again. "I have no idea what it's like to lose someone you love, and I *can't* imagine how you feel, but I see how unhappy you are, how desperate, and how you are trying to understand yourself –"

"Don't be stupid! The only reason you're standing here is curiosity. You want to know why I don't have a sunny smile on my face like the others. Well, now I've told you. Who knows why I did that? And now, please, leave me alone! I don't need you! I don't need anyone! The only person who could have helped me is dead! Do you understand? She's dead! Gone! Finished! Just like that. I hate her for doing that!"

"No, you don't!"

"Yes, I do!"

"Caitlin, I don't believe that! You know that there are some diseases that you just can't beat. I'm sure that your mother would have preferred to stay with you!"

"Oh, come on! Stop it! I don't want to talk about it anymore!"

"But it's good for you to talk about it. Sometimes it helps, and –"

"You talk and talk, just like my father. He doesn't understand anything about how I feel!"

Ricki looked at the girl for a long time.

"Have you ever thought that maybe he feels the same way you do inside? After all, he lost his wife. But even so, how is he or anyone else supposed to understand

52

what you're going through when you don't understand yourself?" she asked quietly. "And since you can't understand your own feelings, you withdraw from everyone and everything, pretending that you don't want anyone around. So everyone thinks that you're an arrogant, self-centered brat, but really, you're just sad and desperate, which isn't anyone else's fault! It's not fair to take it out on others, no matter how terrible your situation is."

Caitlin buried her face in her hands. Silently she cried her pain away, unable to think clearly about anything. Everything seemed so senseless to her, and Ricki's words had just confirmed what she'd been reading in the eyes of her former friends for months now. Unhappiness and arrogance were dominant in her life right now, at least on the outside, but Ricki seemed to be the only one to notice and recognize that this was all just a façade, a wall around her heart which she had built in order to hide her true feelings.

"Come here," said Ricki suddenly in a soft voice and pulled the twelve-year-old toward her. Gently, she put her hand under her chin and forced her to look up at her.

"Caitlin, I think I understand you better than you think," whispered Ricki. Carefully, she put her arms around her and rubbed her back, a little awkwardly. "Everything is going to be all right, believe me," she said haltingly. She kept taking deep breaths, trying to say something, but the right words just didn't seem to come. So she was silent and hoped that Caitlin would calm down again.

After what seemed a long time to Ricki, Caitlin got out of her arms and just lay down exhausted on the bed.

"Thanks," she whispered weakly, without opening her eyes. Ricki tried to smile.

"It's okay. I'm going to go down to the others, all right?" She started to get up, but suddenly Caitlin looked at her pleadingly.

"Please, Ricki... please stay." Shivering, she grasped the hand of the fourteen-year-old and held on as though she were drowning.

Ricki swallowed and then she nodded. "Okay, if that's what you really want."

Caitlin nodded gratefully and then she closed her eyes.

When Carlotta opened the door quietly a short time later and peered into the room, she found both girls lying next to each other on the bed, sleeping, and Ricki had put an arm around Caitlin as though to protect her.

I knew I was doing the right thing when I asked you to keep an eye on that girl, Carlotta thought, looking at Ricki with a smile. Then she quietly closed the door behind her.

Chapter 4

"Hey, tell me, what kind of a person is Ricki?" Lena asked Lillian as though it wasn't really that important. The two girls were leaning on Holli's stall door and watching the blacksmith, Leon, as he trimmed the hooves of Sheila, the Black Forest mare.

"What do you mean by that?" Lillian hadn't really been paying attention, because she was fascinated by the way Leon dealt with the obstinate animal.

"Easy, my little sweetie, now stand still a little while longer. It'll be over soon," Cheryl's voice could be heard comforting her foster horse, but Sheila kept pulling her hoof away from her.

"Honey, this isn't going to work! We'll be here till tomorrow!" Leon stood up and grinned at his sweaty helper. "Young people today just don't have any muscle. Can't even hold the hoof of a little horse still for a minute!"

"I could, if Sheila would hold still!" panted Cheryl, out of breath.

"Can I help you?" Hal didn't even wait for Cheryl's answer, but just went and stood beside Sheila.

"So, sweetie, now we're going to show your rider how it's done, okay?" He stroked Sheila's hind leg on a particular spot, before he picked up the back hoof and then put himself in a professional position.

Leon couldn't keep from laughing. "You young guys are always trying to impress the girls! But I don't care who helps me, and I'm curious to see how long Sheila's going to stand still with you holding her hoof!"

"Until we're done," Hal was just about to say, quite sure of himself, when Sheila shifted her entire weight onto Hal and kicked so the boy had to drop the hoof after all.

"Darn it!" Hal gave the horse a slap, which made Leon look at him disapprovingly.

"Why did you do that?"

"She should know that she did something wrong," responded Hal.

"And you think giving her a slap is going to help?"

"A slap? That wasn't a slap! Sheila hardly noticed it!" Hal tried to defend his actions.

"If she hardly noticed it, then it would have been pointless, wouldn't it? And if she did, then from now on she'll associate lifting her hooves with something scary, which means she won't be as eager to let anyone lift her hooves in the future. And if she does, then she'll try to pull it back as fast as possible, since she won't want to be scared again!"

"It's not pointless! She'll associate the slap with her pulling back her hoof!"

Leon shook his head. "No, young man. That's your human brain at work, but horses don't think logically like humans. They can only associate things with the immediate situation," explained the blacksmith, while the kids looked at each other.

"Do you believe that?" Karen asked her brother quietly, but he just shrugged his shoulders and watched closely as Hal made another attempt, which ended just like the first. Hal was fortunate that Sheila's hoof shot past his head when she vented her anger.

"Am I supposed to think that this is okay?" Hal was angry.

The animal laid her ears back flat on her head, while she stared at Hal with rolling eyes.

Leon shook his head. "No, that's not okay, but she hasn't forgotten your slap."

"Maybe it's because Sheila doesn't like men," Cheryl attempted to defend her horse. "I think her previous owner wasn't very kind to her!"

"Then we'll have to be even gentler with her now. Did you say she doesn't like men?" Leon moved next to Cheryl.

"Would you please leave me alone with her for a few minutes?" he asked pleasantly and untied Sheila from the stall.

"Of course, but be careful!" the girl said. "As I said, she –"

"She doesn't like men. I know. Don't worry, Cheryl." Leon smiled and waited until the girl had stepped aside, then he looked at Sheila for a long time without saying anything. The kids heard him speaking very quietly to her, and the animal gave him her full attention and seemed to relax after a few minutes.

"Well? Are you ready? Can we do this?" asked Leon gently, and let the rope drop to the ground.

Cheryl, who saw it fall, wanted to run over immediately, in order to hold Sheila, but Leon waved her away.

"Stand still," he ordered.

"But –"

"Stand still!" he said again, before he bent down to pick up his hoof knife. Then he stepped beside Sheila, who wasn't tied up, and picked up the first hoof.

"Fascinating!" whispered Lillian, and the others in the stable made similar admiring remarks.

Leon was able to pick up one leg after the other without any trouble, and Sheila stood still and relaxed until all of her hooves were trimmed. The blacksmith didn't even need any help. Then he stepped in front of the horse and praised her extravagantly.

"I told you it wouldn't hurt, didn't I? The next time I come, you'll know that, Sheila. Thank you for cooperating so nicely!"

"I just can't believe it," Hal said, shaking his head. "What did you do to her? Did you hypnotize her or something?"

Leon gave him a long look. "You just have to learn to put yourself in the horse's shoes, to try to understand her, her fears, her emotions. Then you have to be calm yourself, so that you can communicate this calmness to the animal. You represent the security that the horse needs in order to become relaxed and reassured. Oh, and then talk to the animal. She understands everything you say."

"I thought horses couldn't think logically, so how can they understand what we say, especially in our language?"

"It doesn't matter which language you speak. The animal understands what you mean through your tone. Communicate to her what you want to say, not only with your voice but also with your feelings. You can be sure that whatever you want to tell her, she'll hear. And Hal, you don't have to hit animals. You'll just achieve the exact opposite of what you want."

58

Slowly, Leon picked up the rope again and held it out to Cheryl. "Here, you can take your horse back to her stall."

"That's unbelievable!" Kevin and Cathy were at least as impressed with Leon as Lillian was.

"So?" Lena piped up, her attention back on Lillian.

"What?"

"Well, you haven't answered my question!"

"What question?" Lillian looked puzzled.

"I wanted to know what kind of a person Ricki is!"

"Oh, yeah. I forgot. Ricki... actually all you have to do is look at her, and then you won't even have to ask," replied Lillian, without thinking.

"That's terrific! Thanks for the info. Now I know everything there is to know." Lena rolled her eyes.

"*Hah,*" Lillian giggled. "Don't look like that. What I said is true. Ricki's a great friend with a generous heart. You can always depend on her and she's always there for you if you need her."

"I see. Is that why she thinks she's better than everyone else?"

"What?" Lillian frowned, taken aback by Lena's remark. "Ricki stuck up? That's the funniest thing I've heard in ages. Why would you think that?"

"I just have that impression. Where is she anyway?"

"I don't know, but if Ricki isn't with Diablo, then there has to be a good reason."

Lena turned toward the huge black horse.

"Diablo," she said dreamily. "It's just too bad he has to belong to Ricki!"

When Lillian heard that, she got really annoyed. "Hey, what's your problem? You don't even know her. Just because

59

she won't let you ride her horse doesn't mean that she's a stuck-up brat."

"I didn't say that!" Lena defended herself.

"But that's what you thought, by the look of you!"

"Well, that's true."

Lillian shook her head.

"Well, at least you're honest, but your bad opinion of someone you don't even know doesn't make you a nice person." With that, she left Lena standing there, and ran over to Kevin and Cathy.

"What's the matter? You look mad!" Cathy noticed Lillian's scowl immediately. She rarely ever saw her friend angry.

"I have a funny feeling that these eight days aren't going to be problem-free," the older girl predicted.

Kevin looked curiously at Lillian. "What do you mean? You've lost me."

"I think Lena's going to make trouble because of Ricki. I have the feeling that she's jealous because Diablo belongs to Ricki."

"That's ridiculous! Lena seems okay," exclaimed Kevin.

"Well, I just hope you're right!"

*

When Ricki woke up from her unplanned nap, she found the bed next to her empty. She immediately sat up and tried to remember the whole conversation with Caitlin.

Whoa, that was pretty intense, what she told me, she said to herself before she left the room.

While she was running down the stairs, she could hear the happy voices of the ranch guests and Kevin's unmistakable laugh coming from the living room.

"Good morning, sleepy head!" Frankie teased her as she came in.

"Ricki, you must be getting old. I don't know how anyone can sleep at this time of day." Cathy grinned.

"You really missed something. The blacksmith hypnotized Sheila!" Kieran slapped his thighs and gave the thumbs-up sign of recognition.

"What? Hypnotized?" Ricki shook her head. She was too sleepy to understand what Kieran was saying. "I think someone hypnotized me as well," she yawned. "Has anyone seen Caitlin?"

"Why are you looking for that witch? She's been ruining everyone's mood!" said Michelle, voicing the common opinion.

Carlotta, who was sitting in her deep armchair, wrinkled her brow. "Michelle, I asked you all to treat everyone with respect!"

"Sorry, Carlotta, but you have to admit that she's not exactly a ray of sunshine, and, strangely, every time she appears, our mood drops down a few notches."

"Exactly!" agreed Bev. "She came in here a while ago just to complain!"

"What was her problem?" asked Ricki, who was by now wide-awake.

"Well, if you must know, she complained that you'd made her mad. Did you?"

Ricki looked incredulously at Bev, before she turned her gaze to Carlotta, who was shaking her head as if to say, *Don't say anything*. So Ricki just cleared her throat loudly and looked up at the ceiling.

"Yeah, I guess so, somehow!" she said, and knew that at

least Kevin, Cathy, and Lillian would know that it wasn't true. "I just didn't want her to feel excluded, and I wanted to talk with her about it, but I guess it didn't work."

"Is it even possible to talk with her?" Hal asked, and then, seeing Carlotta's expression, he quickly added, "Okay, I'm sorry!"

"And where is she now?" Ricki still wanted to know, but no one knew the answer to her question.

"If she's not in her room, she probably went to the stable," Carlotta suggested.

"I thought we weren't supposed to go there alone," said Karen openly.

"Exactly! Carlotta, you said that one of the older kids should always go with us, and that we're not supposed to keep running over to bother the horses because they need some quiet time too," added Patrick.

"Yeah, that's what you said! How come Caitlin is allowed to go to the stable alone? That's not fair!" Frankie, who would have liked to spend all of his time with Silver, was looking at Carlotta with accusing eyes.

"Well, young man, first of all, there's nothing unfair about it, and secondly, each of you has been allowed to select your horse for the week, and Caitlin is probably doing that right now, and thirdly, I gave her permission to go ahead and wait for Ricki there."

"Ohhh, oh yeah, that's right. I'm sorry, Carlotta, I completely forgot that I was supposed to go to the stable with Caitlin. I'm on my way!" Ricki turned on her heel and disappeared before anyone could ask her more questions.

"So, since this issue has been resolved, let's get started on the list of chores," suggested Carlotta. "As I said, we're going to divide the daily chores: cooking, washing, stable. We need two people each day for each chore, three times a day. For the work in the stable, we need four people.

"Well, Kieran and Hal have to help with the cooking too!" Lena giggled.

"And Kevin too! Hey, maybe your mom can lend you an apron," grinned Cathy before she volunteered for the first shift, just to be on the safe side. "I'll volunteer to do the dishes tonight. Who's with me?"

"Me!" Michelle raised her hand. "If I work with you, I won't have to help Caitlin."

"Okay. And who's going to help fix dinner?"

"I think I'll get that over with right away," sighed Kieran.

"Oh, that sounds like fun, Kieran! I'll help you!" Patrick beamed at the older boy, whom he had secretly chosen as his role model.

Carlotta smiled. "And you're probably all going to fight over who gets to do the stable chores this evening, aren't you?"

"I'm going to the stable!" called out Frankie immediately.

"Me, too!" said Kevin right after him.

"Me, too!" shouted Lillian, almost the same time as Lena.

"How nice! At least today is already planned. Now let's take care of the schedule for tomorrow, and when we're finished with that I suggest we make ourselves a big pot of tea and eat this marvelous cake that Kevin's mother baked for us. We can get to know each other a little better while we're eating by telling some things about ourselves," suggested Carlotta, and she looked around at the other faces, all nodding in agreement.

*

"Thanks, Carlotta! Thanks a lot!" grumbled Ricki in a bad mood, as she opened the door to the stable. "You don't spare me anything!" All of the sympathy she'd built up during her conversation with Caitlin was forgotten after she heard that she had supposedly been a bother to the girl.

She slammed the door to the stable a little louder than she'd planned, making all the horses look up curiously as she walked in.

Diablo, who recognized his human immediately, greeted her with a loud whinny. He scraped the straw in his stall impatiently with his front hoof until Ricki finally stood in front of him and patted his outstretched neck.

"Well, boy, did you miss me? Come on, stop digging around in your stall. That doesn't get you anything!"

While she was stroking her horse, Ricki gazed around the stable, but she couldn't find Caitlin anywhere.

"Darn it. Where can she be?"

Diablo looked at her with his big brown eyes.

"Sweetie, I'll be right back. I have to go find Miss Lisser."

The black horse seemed to be insulted that Ricki was leaving him so quickly, but she had hardly left the stable when someone else started to stroke him.

Caitlin, who had hidden herself in one of the corners of his stall, had stood up, and was now stroking Diablo's forehead, right on his white star.

"That was lucky. She didn't see me. Thank you, beautiful, for not giving me away." Caitlin slipped quickly out of Diablo's stall and left the stable through the front entrance so as not to run into Ricki.

When she felt the cold outside, the twelve-year-old had to take a few deep breaths to keep from shivering. Then she pulled her heavy jacket tighter around her and walked away from the ranch as fast as she could through the deep snow. She had no idea where she was going.

"I don't care about any of you!" she said, taking one last look at the stable.

*

After about half an hour, Carlotta looked over at the old clock on the wall above the fireplace. "Kevin, do me a favor and go over to the stable. Tell the girls that they have to tear themselves away from the horses and come back here. Tell them we're waiting for them with tea and cake!"

Ricki's boyfriend jumped up. "Okay, I'll be right back, so save me a piece of cake. Mom's apple cake is my absolute favorite!"

"You're impossible! Don't worry, you'll get your share," joked Lillian.

"Is he always like that?" asked Bev, interested.

"No, he's usually much worse," replied Cathy seriously, and she took a second piece, just to be on the safe side. "If I were you, I'd hurry up. When he gets back and starts eating there won't be anything left. He can eat more than you can even imagine!"

*

Kevin tore open the door to the stable. "Hey, Ricki, you're supposed – Ricki?" Astonished, he stared at the empty corridor. "Hellooo, where are you? In the tack room?... Nope, hmm." Bewildered, the boy stood there for a

65

moment. Just as he was about to run back to the house, Ricki came in, looking a little pale.

"Hey, where were you two? Carlotta sent me. I'm supposed to tell you –"

"Caitlin is gone!" interrupted Ricki.

" – that there's tea and cake. Wait a minute, what did you just say?"

"Caitlin is gone!"

"What do you mean, gone?"

"Just gone! Disappeared! Vanished!"

"No!"

Ricki rolled her eyes. "Do you think I'm kidding? I've been looking all through the stable for about half an hour, in all of the rooms and stalls, and I can't find her!!"

"That's impossible! Did you really look everywhere? Even in the attic? In the hayloft?"

"If I tell you that I looked everywhere, then that's what I did! I can't find her! But where can she be? I mean, surely she wouldn't go home on foot, would she?" Ricki bit her lip. If only she had woken up when Caitlin left the room.

"Come on, come with me. We have to tell Carlotta right away." Kevin grabbed Ricki's hand and together they ran back into the house and right into the happy little group laughing and talking around the table.

"Caitlin is gone!" repeated Ricki, a little louder this time so that her voice could be heard above the others.

Carlotta looked as skeptical as Kevin had a few moments before. "No! What makes you think so?"

"It's true. I've looked everywhere! She's nowhere to be found!"

All of the kids were silent.

"Could it be that Caitlin is just trying to attract attention?" Michelle suggested timidly.

"I can't imagine why she'd do that. You all heard her say that she just wanted to be left alone, so I don't think that she'd want sixteen people looking for her." Carlotta shook her head. "But it is strange that she just went away without telling me."

"So where can she be?" Amy looked worried.

"Anywhere and everywhere," answered Kieran, trying to be funny.

"Terrific! I don't think that was funny at all!" Ricki's eyes blazed.

"Maybe she just went for a walk," Karen offered, turning to Carlotta whose face had suddenly gone pale.

"Yes, that's possible. Let's hope it's true," she answered, as she turned to meet Ricki's gaze.

"Should we start looking for her in the area?"

"No," Carlotta replied firmly. "At least, not yet. I suggest we all search the house first, then the stable and the shed, and try to find places where someone could hide."

"But I already did –"

"Ricki, I know! Nevertheless, let's look everywhere again. We have to find her, even if we have to go through the house ten times! So, let's get going! Search everywhere, including under the beds, behind cupboards, in the basement, just anywhere she could be. We've got to find her, otherwise we've got a big problem."

The kids nodded dejectedly and left the living room immediately to start looking. Only Kieran was still standing in front of Carlotta, hesitating.

"What's wrong with Caitlin? Carlotta, you know more

about the guests than we do, and there's something wrong with that girl, I can feel it!"

"You're right, Kieran," said Carlotta, sighing. "I'll tell you when the time is right. But right now, I think it's more important just to find her."

The boy nodded. "Okay." And with that, he left to join the search as well.

*

Man, it's really cold, thought Caitlin, as her blue lips shivered in the freezing air and her teeth chattered rhythmically.

She wasn't that far away from the ranch yet, and she could still see the smoke rising from the chimney above the tops of the trees. Longingly, she thought of the others, sitting in Carlotta's warm, cozy kitchen, telling jokes and laughing together.

They probably haven't even noticed that I'm gone, she thought. She beat her hands together to warm up her cold fingers and get the blood circulating. *They don't care about me. Not at all! Dad, why did you bring me here in the first place? I didn't want to come! And that Ricki... I told her everything. Oh, why did I do that? She's probably told them everything, and now everyone will look at me with pity... I can't stand it! I want to go home!*

Caitlin could feel her head getting hotter and hotter the colder she got. The snow was so deep that it came up over the tops of her boots. Her pants and socks were already soaking wet, and her whole body felt cold. And when sleet started to fall, Caitlin began to feel as if she were being frozen like an ice cube.

Turn back, her inner voice kept telling her, but the girl decided stubbornly not to listen.

Turn back, home is too far!

"I can do it!" Caitlin tried to convince herself. "I just have to rest a little!"

Without thinking, she sat down on a snowy tree stump at the edge of the woods, which she had finally reached with a great deal of effort.

"I'm just going to close my eyes for a minute," she whispered, completely exhausted, while the cold east wind blew the sleet right into her face and mixed it with her tears.

"Mama... why aren't you here?" she sobbed and she doubled over, shivering.

Chapter 5

"Okay, I agree. Caitlin is missing." Carlotta gazed seriously into the faces of the kids, who appeared to be very upset. "I don't believe that she just decided to take a walk."

"So you think that she decided to walk home?" Ricki shook her head in horror.

Carlotta nodded silently.

"But if she was unhappy here, she could have just called her father to come and pick her up, couldn't she?" Michelle rolled her eyes. "She's more stupid than I thought."

"Michelle, that girl is anything but stupid. She's simply in despair, that's all!" Ricki exploded.

Carlotta took a deep breath. "Okay, actually, I didn't want to tell you this, for Caitlin's sake, but now I think you should know what's going on with her so that you can understand her better. Her mother died of cancer about six months ago, and Caitlin has still not been able to deal with her loss. Her father thought it might take her mind off her grief if she spent a few days here with people her own age who share her interests. He asked me not to tell

70

you anything, because he didn't want you to pity her. Now, however, I think it's important to inform you all, because I've noticed that you're putting Caitlin into a category in which she doesn't belong."

The kids listened silently.

"And you think that she just couldn't stand seeing how happy we all were, while she was still struggling with the death of her mother, and that's why she ran away?" asked Lillian softly.

Carlotta nodded again. "I'd asked Ricki to keep an eye on Caitlin, but the girl has apparently decided to leave before anyone finds out even more about her."

"And what are we going to do now?" Kieran had deep creases in his forehead as he caught Michelle's glance. The twelve-year-old looked extremely upset and ashamed. She had no idea that Caitlin was wrestling with such a big problem.

"I am so sorry for what I said about Caitlin," she said quietly.

"Sometimes you should just keep your mouth shut," Amy said dryly to her sister.

"Oh, why don't you just keep out of it, okay?"

"Mom always says –"

"Keep out of it!"

"Could you two have your family fight another time? I think, at the moment, we have bigger problems!" Cathy interrupted the siblings.

"We could saddle the horses and ride around the area," suggested Ricki.

"In this weather? No, that's out of the question. We'd be frozen solid before we even got into the saddle." Hal began to shiver at the thought that he would have to set foot outside the house in this sleet, never mind ride through the area, just because stupid Caitlin wasn't able to control herself. Ricki sure had some ridiculous ideas!

"I think we should call her father. He should at least know what a mess his daughter's got herself in." Nervously, Kieran kept changing his posture, standing on one leg, and then the other.

"Well, I think before we make the man crazy, we should try to find her ourselves," commented Kevin. "I'll go with you, Ricki. Anybody else?"

Lillian and Cathy both stepped up spontaneously, and Cheryl looked at Carlotta questioningly. "Can I ride Sheila?"

Carlotta struggled with herself. On the one hand, she didn't feel good about the kids riding out on their horses in this weather, but, on the other hand, she didn't see any other course of action if they were to find Caitlin.

"Hmm. Sheila doesn't have horseshoes and neither does Rashid. How about your horses?"

"Diablo has calkins on his horseshoes, which are good for traction," Ricki answered quickly.

"Holli does, too," nodded Lillian and looked at Kevin anxiously.

"Sharazan doesn't have horseshoes, as you know."

"Okay, kids, then let's go." Carlotta had made her decision. "But please, for heaven's sake, dress warmly: thick jackets, mittens, hoods –"

"Yes, Mommy!" Kevin grinned tolerantly.

"Hey, I want to ride, too!" announced Michelle.

"Me, too," could suddenly be heard from all sides, but Carlotta shook her head.

"No! You are all going to ride, but not today. First of all, you don't know the area; secondly, you aren't familiar with the horses yet; and thirdly, I don't want you all coming back completely frozen. No, you others are staying here with me!"

"Oh, man!" Lena made a pouting face.

"Come on!" Ricki was already on her way to the door when Carlotta's voice held her back once again.

"Ricki, I know you and I know your desire to find Caitlin, no matter what it takes. Nevertheless, I want to ask you to be back here in no longer than an hour and a half. I don't want to have to worry about you, too. And don't take any risks. If you see that the ground is frozen and your horses are sliding, turn back immediately!"

"Of course, Carlotta. Don't worry, we'll be careful, and we'll be back long before we start to freeze, I promise." Ricki strode out of the room, followed by her friends.

"Good luck," murmured Carlotta. "I hope you find her."

*

About twenty minutes later, the five friends, warmly dressed, mounted their horses.

Carlotta and the others stood at the windows and watched them leave until they disappeared in the thick snow that was beginning to come down again.

"I hope I was right to let them ride off. At least the sleet has stopped." Carlotta was startled by the touch of a hand on her shoulder.

"Don't worry," said Bev. "They'll come back safely, and I'm sure they'll find Caitlin."

Carlotta swallowed hard and turned away. The kids had no idea what she was thinking right now. After all, it was

73

the first time she had guests at Mercy Ranch, and already, on the day they arrived, there was a crisis. *What will the remaining seven days be like?* Carlotta wondered. At the moment, she wasn't so sure it had been a good idea to offer riding vacations. She felt a tremendous responsibility for the young guests that had been entrusted to her care. And now Caitlin had disappeared, and she had to hope that Ricki and her friends would find her.

Lena had stared after the riders as well and focused on Diablo, until she couldn't see him anymore.

Someday I'm going to ride that horse, Ricki, whether you like it or not, she vowed to herself. *If it's the last thing I do, I am going to sit in the saddle of that wonderful horse at least once!*

"Hey, what kind of a look is that? You look like you want to jump on someone," teased Kieran, and poked her in the side. "Admit it, you'd have liked to go with them. Me too, but honestly, I don't envy them out there freezing their rear ends off."

"Yeah, yeah," replied Lena, without really listening to her fellow volunteer ranch hand. Her thoughts were on Diablo.

*

Caitlin couldn't feel her feet anymore and she stumbled through the snowy winter woods, her eyes wide open and focused on the white ground. She felt an enormous heat rising within her, while her body shivered in the cold. With one jerk, she took off her scarf.

This thing is making me crazy! she thought, and tied the scarf loosely around her waist. Then she stumbled on. For the last few minutes the girl was beginning to feel dizzy. She kept

74

shaking her aching head. Her hair was covered with icicles. No matter how much she shook her head, however, the snow and the whole area began to shimmer before her eyes.

What's going on? she wondered and she felt her heart beating wildly. *Why can't I see anything clearly?*

She screamed, but not loudly. "Everything just looks like gray spots!" She looked around in panic and then looked up at the sky. It didn't look as if the snowstorm was going to stop anytime soon.

"I'm going crazy," she whispered. She closed her eyes tight, and wished that this was just a dream, but when she opened her eyes again the shimmering spots seemed even worse.

Caitlin's eyes began to burn and water.

"Oh my gosh, what is this? It can't be?"

She looked all around frantically, but she couldn't recognize anything clearly.

Caitlin raised her hands and pressed them against her face. She had the feeling that her fear was making her crazy. Thousands of stars danced around her and robbed her of any visibility.

"I want to go home," Caitlin shouted and turned around in a circle, unsure of where she was. It was no longer possible to recognize any direction, and she sank to her knees sobbing. Her nerves were stretched to the breaking point. What in the world had she been thinking when she just ran off in this awful weather?

*

"She can't have gotten very far." Lillian's voice was barely audible. She had wrapped her long wool scarf around her head several times.

"Brrrr! It's unbelievably cold! I don't know if it was

75

such a good idea to go off with the horses. Rashid is sliding as though he were wearing ice skates! I don't feel good about this anymore," piped up Cathy, and Kevin and Cheryl both looked equally worried.

"That's true. The ground around here is totally frozen and icy."

"We should go back!"

Ricki reined in Diablo gently and turned around to face her friends. "Hmm, with the calkins it's not so bad, don't you think, Lily?"

"Yeah, Holli isn't having any problems."

The five friends looked at each other, trying to decide what to do.

"I suggest that Lily and I ride a bit farther, and you guys can turn back before something happens," said Ricki, shivering from the cold.

"You're completely frozen, too. Don't you want to go back home with us?"

"No. I'm guessing that once we get into the woods, where it isn't so windy, it won't be so bad."

"Whatever you say."

"Okay, see you later. I'll be glad when Sheila gets off this ice," admitted Cheryl, and turned her horse carefully.

Ricki and Lillian waited until their friends were on their way back before they started off on Diablo and Holli. Soon the trees protected them somewhat from the storm, but they were going at a snail's pace.

"If only we knew where to look," complained Lillian inside her scarf. "It's possible that she went in a completely different direction. What a bummer! It won't stop snowing! Otherwise we could have followed her footprints."

"But where else could she be besides in the woods? If she were out on the fields, we'd have seen her by now. Anyway, if she's heading for home, then this is the only place she could be," answered Ricki.

"Yeah, you're right, provided of course that she actually ran away and isn't hiding somewhere on the ranch."

"Come on, we looked everywhere! She wasn't there!"

"Well, at least it didn't look like it. If she hid behind a bale of hay, then we would have had to clear out the entire hayloft, just to be sure."

"Gee, Lillian, you really know how to cheer a person up!" Ricki rolled her eyes, but secretly she had to admit that her friend was right. It was possible that they were wasting their time searching for her off the ranch.

"You don't feel like looking for her anymore, do you?"

"An honest answer? Not really! It was stupid to start out in the first place."

"Then why did you come with me?"

"Oh, Ricki, don't be mad."

"I mean, you knew that it was cold out here. But maybe we'll still find Caitlin."

Lillian looked at her doubtfully. "Do you really believe that?"

"Oh, I don't know, but I hope so. Especially for Carlotta's sake."

Lillian nodded silently and was a little ashamed. She had forgotten about the difficulties the owner of Mercy Ranch would face if Caitlin wasn't found soon.

"You're right. Okay, let's go. We'll ride as far as possible, as long as we can stand it, back and forth through the woods, and shout as loud as we can. If Caitlin is really there, she'll answer us for sure. She'll be even colder than we are."

77

Determined, Lillian urged Doc Holliday forward, and Ricki was glad that her friend had decided to ride with her instead of returning to the warmth and comfort of Mercy Ranch.

*

Carlotta had retreated into her little office and was struggling with herself. *Maybe it wouldn't have gotten this far if I hadn't talked to her like that in the stable,* she thought. *Why didn't I just let her go back home with her father, as she wanted?*

She stared at the telephone for a few seconds before grabbing the receiver firmly. As unpleasant as it would be, she couldn't avoid it any longer. She had to tell Mr. Lisser that his daughter had disappeared.

Carlotta sighed deeply and dialed his number. She had already figured out what she was going to say, and now she waited for Caitlin's father to pick up. The phone, however, kept ringing and ringing. Mr. Lisser didn't seem to be home.

She tried to reach Caitlin's father every few minutes after that for about half an hour, but then she gave up.

She paced back and forth in her office and held on to the hope that Ricki and her friends would find the girl uninjured and bring her back. If Caitlin made it back to Mercy Ranch it would be so much easier to tell Mr. Lisser everything.

She breathed heavily and once again reached for the phone and dialed Caitlin's father. "Please, kids, find her," she whispered quietly toward the window.

*

In the meantime, Hal and Kieran had sawed up a few boards that were left over from the renovation, and now they carried them, along with sandpaper, pencils, and paint, into Carlotta's kitchen, where the campers looked at them in anticipation.

"Is that for firewood?" Frankie pointed at the boards.

"No, we're going to make a hamster cage," winked Hal.

"A hamster cage? Really, we are? Does somebody here have a hamster?"

"No, we're not building a cage. I was just kidding. We thought that since you're the first guests at the ranch, you could paint the name plaques for your horses. That way, there will always be a permanent reminder of your visit, because once the signs are hung up they're here to stay!" Kieran gazed around the group, beaming, and tried to cheer everyone up, but it wasn't going too well.

"Really? Forever?" asked Amy, looking at Kieran.

"Of course! Or let's say, at least as long as the horses are here at Mercy Ranch," he limited it a little, but Karen just disregarded his last sentence.

"So, forever! Great, but I've got lousy handwriting. No one will be able to read it, or at least that's what my mom says."

"And the signs are supposed to be decorated, too, aren't they? In art, I got a D!" whined Patrick.

"Oh, no! Do we have to?" Michelle groaned as well.

"Man, you guys are a lazy bunch!" Bev scolded them, grinning.

"We can make stencils for the letters and the decorations, and then they'll all be the same," suggested Cathy, and for that she got a nasty look from Kieran.

"I think it would be more fun if each sign had its own look."

"Well, I think it's a great idea!" Frankie beamed. "Can we change the plaque shapes a little with a jigsaw?"

"What? You and a jigsaw?" Hal shook his head firmly.

"Your parents would kill us if anything happened to you! Oh no, let's not get into saws!"

"Oh, come on, then at least we could say which form we'd like to have, and you could saw them into that shape, couldn't you?"

Kieran grinned. "As long as you don't completely break the saw, it's okay!"

Hal took a deep breath and resigned himself. "Okay! Then everybody take a board and a pencil and draw the outline you want, and also just sketch in the name of the horse so that we can see what the sign will look like when it's finished."

"Couldn't we use stencils after all?" Michelle tried one last time, and then glared at her sister moodily when she handed her a piece of wood.

"Don't make such a big deal out of it! We all want to see how you can't draw," giggled Amy.

"It's better not to be able to draw than to be so stupid like you!" countered the older sister immediately.

"Don't you dare say that I'm stupid again!"

"Even if it's true?"

"You are so mean!"

"It's your own fault! You started it!" Michelle turned away and decided just to ignore her little sister for the rest of the week.

"Little sisters are so annoying," she sighed, winking sweetly at Hal.

"Big sisters, too," he responded, laughing, and winked at Amy, who had already regretted a hundred times that she hadn't been allowed to come here by herself.

"Well thanks a lot!" grumbled Michelle, and she grabbed a pencil and got to work, thinking, *Hadrian will have a horse fit when he sees my sign on his box.*

*

When Carlotta heard the click of the connecting door to the stable, she got up quickly and almost stumbled over Gandalf and Lucky, who had curled up at her feet.

"Heavens, can't you two be careful?" she yelled, just able to catch herself from falling.

The two dogs raised their heads and looked at her questioningly.

Carlotta took a deep breath, and then she bent down and gently stroked the animals' soft coats.

"I'm sorry. It was my fault," she said, more friendly now, but then she left the room quickly.

"Did you find her?" she asked immediately when she saw Kevin, but he just shook his head dismally.

"No, not yet. Cathy, Cheryl, and I had to turn back. The horses were sliding too much."

Carlotta turned pale. "And what about Ricki and Lillian? Don't tell me they kept on going?"

Kevin nodded.

"Don't worry. Diablo and Holli were the only ones who didn't have a problem with the ground," he tried to console Carlotta, but she just shook her head firmly.

"It's too dangerous! I should never have allowed them to go. I should never have allowed any of you to go!"

"But it's the only shot at finding Caitlin, isn't it?"

"I shouldn't have allowed it," Carlotta said and started to get her jacket off the hook.

"What are you going to do?"

"I'm going to get into my car and drive after them."

Kevin held his breath and stood in her way.

"Carlotta, you won't get far, and anyway, if you slid into a ditch, what would we do? I mean, you're in charge of everything here!"

"I have a responsibility to the girls! Get out of my way, please!"

Kevin stood firm. "You're also responsible for the other kids! If something happens to you –"

Carlotta pushed Kevin aside.

"And if something happens to the three out there, I'll never forgive myself!" she said, and stamped out of the house.

Kevin looked at her with concern. *Terrific*! he thought, and then he ran after her.

"Carlotta, wait! I'm coming with you!" he called and jumped into her car before she had a chance to turn the key in the ignition.

"Please, go back inside the house!"

"No!"

"Kevin, get out!"

"No! Just imagine what will happen if your tires start to skid. You'll be glad to have a strong man with you who can help push the car!"

Carlotta rolled her eyes. "All right then, let's go."

She tried to start the old car, but after it made a choking sound twice, the car was silent.

"Frozen!" guessed Kevin, and he breathed a sigh of relief. "Carlotta, you can forget about it. It's not going to start again today."

Frustrated, the woman beat the palm of her hand against the steering wheel. "Stupid car! Now what?"

"Now we're going back in and waiting for the others to get back. I don't think they'll be able to stand the cold much longer anyway," replied Kevin. Carlotta tried one last time to start the car, but it barely made a sound.

She got out angrily and slammed the door. She gazed intently over the unending whiteness of the landscape.

"Kevin, please saddle Cora for me."

"WHAT?" The youth turned pale.

"I want you to saddle Cora! Are your ears clogged?" Carlotta hobbled determinedly back to the house, leaning on her cane.

"You want to ride after them? On Cora? Carlotta, you can't do that!" shouted Kevin, completely beside himself.

"Why not? Have you forgotten that I can ride?"

"But you haven't been on a horse since your accident, and that's... how many years ago?"

"At least a hundred! Go on and saddle that horse! I'll be back in five minutes."

"But –"

"You don't forget how to ride, even after an accident. I can't perform on horseback anymore, but I can still sit in the saddle. Now, hurry up, boy!" With these words, she disappeared into the house to get changed.

Kevin hurried to the stable. He knew that he wouldn't be able to get Carlotta to change her mind.

"So stubborn! Unbelievable!" he murmured to himself, and a short time later he was buckling the saddle girth and the snaffle.

Cora held her gray spotted head toward him and watched Kevin work. She had no idea how awful the weather outside was, and seemed happy at the prospect of being ridden again.

"What are you doing?" Cathy and Cheryl were standing in front of the stall looking at their friend in disbelief.

"She wants to ride after the others on Cora and look for them!"

"What?"

"Who?"

"Carlotta!" Slowly, Kevin turned around.

"Don't be ridiculous!" Just as Kevin had earlier, Cathy turned pale. "She hasn't ridden for ages!"

"And Cora doesn't have horseshoes. She'll slide just as much as our horses did."

"I know, but her mind is made up!" Kevin shrugged his shoulders. He didn't feel comfortable with Carlotta's plan, and the other two girls were already thinking with horror about what could happen.

"Are you finished?" he heard Carlotta's voice coming from the stable door. The clack of the cane on the cement floor could be heard as well.

"Yeah, but –"

"Fine, then I can get started!" Carlotta leaned her cane against the outer wall of the stall and grabbed Cora's reins.

"Don't you want to think this over?" asked Cathy quietly.

"There's nothing to think about. Now, don't worry. Cora is really gentle. She's perfect for old ladies who want to ride around in the snow."

"It's not the snow that worries us. It's the ice. Cora's going to slide," exclaimed Cheryl.

"That's exactly what's bothering me, too! The ice! Why do you think I want to go?" asked Carlotta, somewhat angrily, and then she led Cora outside. "I won't feel right until your friends are back, safe and sound. Now, let me go, and, please, shut the stable door after me. Keep an eye on the others, and... no one has to know what I'm doing. Our guests

84

are supposed to be enjoying happy, fun-filled days on the ranch. When Caitlin is back, they'll forget about the whole thing fairly quickly." Carlotta pulled the saddle girth tighter once more, and then she turned one last time to Kevin.

"Kevin, I've tried to reach Mr. Lisser for over an hour, to tell him about Caitlin's disappearance, but he doesn't seem to be home. Keep trying to reach him while I'm gone. If you get him on the line, tell him he should come to the ranch immediately. I know, Kevin, that this isn't an easy task for you, but please do it anyway. The man has to know what's going on. The telephone number is on my desk under the glass paperweight."

Kevin nodded, although the thought of having to give Mr. Lisser the bad news made him very uncomfortable.

"You can count on me, Carlotta. I'll keep dialing until I reach him," he promised solemnly.

"Thank you, Kevin. I know I can depend on you. Okay, then, see you all later!" Faster than the friends had thought possible, Carlotta was in the saddle and leaving the yard.

"I hope nothing goes wrong," whispered Cathy nervously as she and the others watched Carlotta and Cora disappear into the thickly falling snow.

Chapter 6

"Caitlin! CAITLIN! Where are you?" Lillian's voice was swallowed by the heavy snow. "I'm going to fall right out of the saddle from shivering so much!"

Ricki glanced over at her girlfriend and had to admit that she didn't feel much better. Nevertheless, she just couldn't give up and turn back. If Caitlin really was walking around somewhere in the woods, they had to find her. She must be almost frozen to death by now.

"Ricki, let's go back. I can't stand this anymore. The cold is really getting to me!"

"Just ten more minutes, okay? She has to be here somewhere. Maybe she's fallen and can't walk."

"Why do you always have to think of the worst-case scenario?"

"I don't," Ricki defended herself. "But you have to admit that it's possible, and if we ride back now –"

"Okay, okay. Ten more minutes. But then we're going home. I really can't take much more of this." Lillian didn't look that great, and Ricki asked herself if she should even make her stay ten more minutes to keep looking. But then she thought of Caitlin again, and she urged Diablo onward. They just had to find the girl.

"CAITLIN!" she screamed in the hope that she would get an answer, but there was only silence. All she could hear was the sound of hooves in the snow.

*

"Oh, I can't do it! I don't have any talent at all!" The kids were sitting in front of their boards, which had been sawed into the desired shapes, and they were trying to write the names of the horses neatly and nicely on the signs.

"Oh, Michelle, you're really getting on my nerves." Kieran looked at her work over her shoulder. "That's not bad at all. I don't know what your problem is!"

"Do you think so?" The girl fluttered her eyelashes at the older boy.

"Hah!" laughed Amy. "She's just saying that so someone will tell her how good her sign looks. She always does that –"

"Shut up!"

"You can't stop me from doing anything! Mom says that you always try to get out of things by saying that you aren't good at them. And now you're hoping that Kieran will draw your letters so that all you have to do is paint them," she responded. "Anyway, you're in love with Kieran!"

Michelle turned bright red at her sister's words, but before she found an appropriate answer, Kevin, Cathy, and Cheryl came into the kitchen, followed by Gandalf and Lucky who sat down right in front of Frankie and Patrick so that the boys would pet them.

87

"I'd love to have a dog," said Patrick, and his eyes took on a dreamy expression.

"I have one at home. He's a dachshund, but he's very funny. He loves tennis balls and socks!" Frankie shook with laughter just remembering how his mother had run through the garden, chasing after Toby to retrieve two new socks he had stolen out of a laundry basket filled with clean clothes.

"Where's Carlotta? I have to ask her something," Hal called to Kevin when he saw him come in.

"What do we tell them?" Cathy whispered to the boy.

"Uhmm, Carlotta just ran into us. She said she wanted to rest for a while before we start on the stable," lied Kevin, crossing his fingers behind his back.

"Oh, is she feeling okay?" Amy was suddenly all ears and the other kids looked up at Kevin and his friends expectantly.

"Sure, sure," countered Cheryl. "It's just that she got up so early this morning, and she's been working until late at night the last few days, preparing for this week so that your stay here would go smoothly!"

"Oh! Well, anyway, she'll really be surprised when she sees the signs we made. They're going to be great!" exclaimed Patrick and held his at arm's length for inspection.

"Yeah, especially Michelle's," Amy teased and received a dirty look from her older sister, who was still mad at her because of the remark about Kieran.

"When are we going to the stable?" Frankie nagged. He was missing Silver again.

"I think in about an hour," replied Bev, glancing at her watch.

"I just hope Carlotta is back by then," Cathy whispered to Cheryl as the two left the kitchen to change into dry clothes. Kevin followed them close behind. He was going to go to Carlotta's office and try his luck with Mr. Lisser.

"Cross your fingers that the guy is finally home," he said to the two girls before disappearing behind the office door.

*

Soaking wet, chilled to the bone, her clothing frozen stiff as a board, Caitlin stood leaning on a tree stump, her eyes wide open.

Her head was hot and she couldn't think clearly anymore. The world seemed to be spinning around her. The humming noise in her ears was becoming louder and louder, and she felt as though she were wrapped in cotton.

Large snowflakes danced down to the ground, and the snow was falling so heavily that it was impossible to see farther than about twenty feet.

"What is that?" whispered Caitlin. She thought she saw the outline of someone who was shining so brightly that it seemed to break through the thick cloud of cotton that engulfed her.

"Who are you? What do you want from me?" Frightened, the girl pressed closer to the tree stump, but when she recognized who was coming toward her, her knees gave way and she collapsed. Caitlin couldn't do anything to stop this person it even if she had wanted to.

"Linnie," she heard a gentle, loving voice say, and it made her heart skip a beat. "Linnie" – how often had she heard this nickname and rolled her eyes in disgust? She thought it was childish to be called by that name, but now –

The spectral vision came closer and closer to the girl, and when it had almost reached her...

Mama! That was the last thing in her thoughts before she lost consciousness.

*

"The snow is getting thicker, Ricki. We have to go back before we get lost!" Lillian wiped her eyes to prevent her eyelashes and eyebrows from freezing to tiny icicles.

Ricki nodded. "Okay. I don't think we're going to find Caitlin now, anyway. Who knows, maybe she really did hide somewhere on the ranch."

"Finally you're at least willing to accept that possibility. Come on! Let's go home!" Lillian was just about to turn Doc Holliday when she froze.

"What's that?"

"What do you mean?" asked Ricki, as she followed the direction of Lillian's gaze.

"That thing over there. What's hanging in those branches?"

"I don't know. Let's take a look." Ricki rode closer and gave a low whistle when she recognized the scarf. "That belongs to Caitlin. She was wearing it when she arrived at the ranch. Lillian, you know what that means? She was here! She has to be nearby. I doubt she could have gotten much farther."

Lillian dismounted and retrieved the scarf, and then she stared at the ground.

"I'm not a Girl Scout or anything, but with a little imagination, I can almost recognize traces of shoe prints!" she said hesitantly.

"Really?" Ricki slipped down from the saddle and looked closely at the faint tracks. "Let's follow them."

While the two girls walked with their horses, struggling through the deep snow, they kept calling loudly to Caitlin, but all around them there was nothing but silence.

"Darn it! I can't see anything anymore," Lillian said after a while. "The snow has completely covered the tracks."

Ricki stood still and put her hands on her hips. She just couldn't accept the idea that their search had been in vain.

"She has to be here somewhere!" she said to cheer herself up, and suddenly she jerked.

"Mama, where are you?"

The two girls looked at other in total shock. The voice they heard was coming from somewhere nearby.

"I knew it! Come on!" Ricki pulled Diablo forward, and he wasn't at all pleased. "Don't be difficult, boy! CAITLIN... WHERE ARE YOU?" she shouted, looking around her, but there was no answer. Then suddenly...

"Darn!" exploded Ricki, and stared at the ground to her right.

"Stop a minute!" she yelled, throwing Diablo's reins to Lillian. Then, rushing a few feet forward, she came to a halt and knelt in the snow. "We've found her, Lillian! She's lying here! What should we do now?" Ricki's voice sounded shrill.

Lillian pulled the two horses behind her. Upon seeing Caitlin's pale face, she was terrified. "Is... is she still alive?"

"I don't know." Ricki grabbed the girl around the shoulders and shook her. "Caitlin!" she screamed at her. "Caitlin! Come on! Wake up!"

"Ricki, don't hurt her!"

"Caitlin! You're not going to die here! Do you hear me? Caitlin!" Ricki was beside herself with worry. Quickly, she took off one of her mittens and slapped the girl a few times with her hand.

Come on, come on, come on! she pleaded silently to the snow-covered figure lying in front of her. She thought her heart would stop beating when, after what seemed like an eternity, a faint shiver ran through Caitlin's body.

"Yes!" exclaimed Ricki. "Caitlin! Can you hear me? Caitlin!" Cautiously, she stroked the girl's face with a trembling hand, and then, with tremendous effort, she raised her up into a sitting position and knelt behind her to support her back. Her arms were wrapped tightly around the girl's upper body, while she tried to rub a little warmth into her to get her circulation moving again.

Caitlin's eyelids fluttered a little and then slowly and with great difficulty they opened a bit. "Mama," she breathed and stared straight ahead. "Mama –"

"Caitlin! It's us! Ricki and Lillian! Are you okay? Hey, answer me!"

"Where are you?" Caitlin's voice was just a slight whisper.

"Here, right next to you!" said Ricki. "We're going to take you home now, okay?"

"Home... Mama..." Exhausted, the girl closed her eyes, but Ricki shook her firmly again.

"No, Caitlin! Don't go to sleep again! Do you hear me? You have to stay awake! Lillian, we have to get her back to the ranch as fast as possible!" Ricki looked at her girlfriend frantically.

"Yeah, but how? We'll never get her up on a horse! She'll collapse before we even get her into the saddle, and how can I help you bring her back? I have to hold onto the horses!"

"Come on. Stop talking! It just has to work! Come over here."

Lillian brought Diablo and Holli as close as possible to the tree stump where Caitlin was sitting. She grabbed Caitlin's arm and Ricki tried with all her might to get the girl up, but they could see that it just wasn't going to work. Caitlin hung in Ricki's arms like a dead weight, and it seemed unlikely that they would be able to lift her up onto a horse.

Panting, Ricki let her sink down to the ground again.

"This just can't be! Now that we've finally found her, we can't get her home! This is just unbelievable! Can you tie up the horses somewhere?"

"Where? The branches on these trees are so high I can't reach them!"

Diablo scraped in the snow with his hoof with boredom, and then he shook himself to get the snow off his coat. Ricki knew that her horse liked winter and enjoyed racing around in the snow, but today it looked like it was just too much, even for him.

"What are we going to do now?"

"That's the question of the year. And the answer is, I have no idea!" Resigned and freezing, Lillian leaned against Holli, whose head shot up all of a sudden. He stared at the gray wall of falling snow intently, and Diablo's ears went back and forth attentively as if he was trying to pick up a scent or a sound.

"Calm down! There's nothing there!" Lillian tugged at the reins, but the animals wouldn't be distracted. Suddenly, Diablo whinnied loudly, which startled all three of them.

Ricki held Caitlin even more tightly. "Don't be afraid,

that was only Diablo. Stay calm," she said and looked accusingly at her black horse.

*

Carlotta had left the ranch on Cora, heading in the same direction she had seen the other riders disappear a long while ago.

She'd been gone for quite some time, and she didn't even know if she would find the girls. But it was better to be out looking for them than just sitting around at home doing nothing but worrying.

Cora moved very cautiously through the snow, almost as though she knew that she didn't dare fall down with Carlotta in the saddle.

"You're such a good girl," Carlotta praised the mare, which felt her way, step by step, nodding her head.

The sun had given up trying to penetrate the thick wall of falling snowflakes, and Carlotta knew that she didn't dare ride much longer and should be thinking about turning back. It was only a matter of time before it would start getting dark.

She gazed intently all around her, but it was impossible to see more than a few feet.

Cora, who had gone this far at a slow pace, stopped all of a sudden and raised her head attentively.

"What's wrong? Don't you feel like going any farther?" Carlotta asked, and pressed her calf gently into the horse's belly, but the animal didn't respond to her urging. "Cora, you're not going to leave me in the lurch, are you? If you stay here, we'll have to spend the night! So come on, let's go, that's a good girl!"

Cora's ears moved back and forth. She was sensing much more than just the words of her rider. She whinnied quietly and then started to move all by herself.

"Slow down, slow down, old girl! We don't want to have an accident! What's wrong? Don't tell me you've caught the scent of your stable mates? Sweetheart, you'll get an extra portion of carrots if you've found Ricki and Lillian! I promise!" Carlotta sat up a little straighter in the saddle and stared in the direction in which Cora was going. All of sudden, she heard the greeting whinnies of one of the geldings herself.

Carlotta's heart jumped. *Thank goodness*, she thought, and looked up at the sky for an instant, before she began to call loudly, "Ricki! Lillian! Where are you? Hello!"

*

"Did you hear that?" Ricki's head turned around suddenly and she stared at Lillian.

"Nope! What?"

"Somebody just called out!"

"What do you mean, 'called out'?"

"Someone called our names. There, again! If I didn't know better, I'd say it was Carlotta's voice." Ricki was still holding Caitlin's limp body in her arms, and by now she could hardly move. She seemed to be frozen solid, but although she was chilled to the bone she still tried to give Caitlin at least a tiny bit of warmth from her own body.

"Carlotta? Are you crazy? I think you're beginning to hallucina – Just a minute! Now I hear it, too!" Lillian took a deep breath, held tightly to the reins, and answered, "Carlotta, over here! We're over here! Hello, hello, here!"

Diablo and Holli had been startled by Lillian's shouting, but the girl held them tightly.

"Don't panic! It's just me!" she spoke comfortingly to the horses and waited a moment before she called out to Carlotta again.

Although only a few minutes had gone by, it seemed like an eternity to Ricki and Lillian until Carlotta and her horse slowly appeared in front of them.

"Heavens, I am so glad I found you!" Carlotta gushed with relief. "If Cora hadn't – My goodness, you've found Caitlin! How is she?" Carlotta dismounted quickly from her horse and handed Lillian the reins before she hobbled hurriedly to the girls.

"Hey, little girl, are you okay? Are you injured?" Worried, Carlotta knelt in the snow and stroked Caitlin's face gently.

"She's awake but she doesn't respond to any questions," said Ricki softly. "She keeps talking about her –"

"Mama, I want to go home..." It was clearly difficult for Caitlin to speak.

"It's okay, Caitlin! I'm here! I'll take you home!" answered Carlotta softly.

"I'm here!" she repeated firmly before she got to her feet again.

"We wanted to lift her up onto a horse, but we couldn't do it," explained Lillian dejectedly.

"How long has she been lying here?"

"We don't know. We've been here for about ten minutes, but there's no telling how long she's been here. She was lying here when we arrived and discovered her just by chance. There was a light, and the –"

Carlotta gestured for Lillian to stop her explanation. "You can tell me all about it later. I think we'll manage to get her up into the saddle. Ricki, take over the horses. Lillian is bigger, and it'll be easier for her than it is for you. Wait. Let's stand Caitlin up on her feet first! Good grief, she's soaking wet!"

"Okay!" With their combined strength Ricki and Carlotta pulled the exhausted girl to her feet. While Carlotta held her up, Ricki took the horses and Lillian stepped over to Carlotta.

"Let's put her on Cora. She's not so tall," decided Carlotta and indicated to Ricki that she should bring the horse closer to them.

"Don't you think that it will be too heavy for old Cora when the two of you are on her back?" asked Lillian, but Carlotta just smiled.

"Don't worry, Cora is used to more than you think! She used to be a transport horse, and I'm sure she carried more pounds around than Caitlin and I weigh together. So, Lillian, here goes!"

*

"It's going to be dark soon, and they're still not back! I'm really worried!" Cathy stood at the window and stared outside while Cheryl hopped from one leg to the other impatiently, hardly listening when one of the guests asked her something.

"Look. How do you like these little curlicues around the first letter?" Karen tugged once again on Cheryl's sleeve.

"Great!" the older girl answered without even looking at the younger girl's work.

"But you didn't even look at it!"

"Yes I did, a while ago!"

"But now it looks completely different!"

Cheryl sighed and finally turned toward the ten-year-old. "I'm sorry. I was just lost in my thoughts. Show me! Oh, that is really a work of art! Honest! I've never seen such a beautiful name plate!"

Karen beamed. "Really?"

"Absolutely!" answered Cheryl and she didn't even have to lie.

"I'm going to become a sign painter for horse stalls!" announced Karen loudly and ran back to her seat to give the last few touches to the lavishly drawn letters.

"Stall sign painter! That's stupid! That doesn't even exist!" Patrick grinned at his sister.

"Then I'll just have to invent it!"

"Yeah, sure! Hey, Kieran, are we going to the stable now?"

Kieran looked up and shook his head. "Did you forget? The two of us have to help with dinner tonight. I think it's only a matter of time until Mrs. Thomas arrives."

Patrick pouted. "Darn it! I completely forgot. But we can at least go into the stable and look, can't we?"

"Oh, yes, please!" The other kids wanted to at least say goodnight to their horses.

"I think we should wait until after dinner," suggested Kevin, hoping that Carlotta would be back by then with the others. He still hadn't been able to reach Caitlin's father.

"Oh, that's not for a long time yet!" Amy looked jealously at Frankie, who wasn't bothered by Kevin's answer, since he was scheduled to work in the stable and would therefore have more chances of giving Silver a carrot.

"Say, shouldn't Ricki and, what's her name, Lillian, be back by now?" asked Michelle suddenly.

"Exactly! And what's going on with Caitlin? What will happen if they don't find her?" Patrick wanted to know.

Kevin, Cathy, and Cheryl exchanged brief looks with Hal and Kieran.

"I think they'll be back soon," Kevin said, trying to be reassuring. "After all, they've been gone long enough, and they know that they have to be back in the stable before dark."

"Yeah, but what about Caitlin?" Patrick insisted, and suddenly it was quiet in Carlotta's kitchen.

Be careful what you say, thought Cathy and searched desperately in her brain for the right words. She thought of Carlotta, who had made it clear to the young ranch hands that they should not upset the guests anymore than they had to.

"Well, I think... I mean... well, I'm pretty sure that Ricki and Lillian have found her," she stumbled.

"Do you really think so?"

Cathy sighed. "I don't know," she said then, very quietly. "But I really hope so! After all, Caitlin can't have disappeared into thin air!"

"Shouldn't Carlotta call the police or at least tell Caitlin's father, instead of lying in bed?" Michelle suddenly asked a little nastily, one eyebrow raised. "I mean, how can the woman just go to bed when one of her guests has disappeared? She's really making it easy on herself. She sent five riders out in this weather, and –"

"Michelle, I think it would be better if you just didn't say

99

any more! You have no idea what you're talking about!" interrupted Kevin angrily. "Anyway, we volunteered to look for Caitlin! I'm sure you could tell that Carlotta didn't really want us to go! And I think Carlotta knows who she needs to tell!"

"Why should I shut up? You act as if nothing happened, and then you make us draw these stupid name plates, as though everything is all right."

"I think that we should call the police," began Amy, who for once agreed with her older sister.

"Hey, you, be quiet! You don't even know how to write the word 'police'!" Michelle hadn't even noticed that Amy had wanted to support her.

"I don't think anyone will be helped if we just sit around here, down in the dumps, twiddling our thumbs and waiting for Carlotta to return. That's not what your parents paid for when they sent you here for a horse vacation," Bev tried to calm everyone down.

"Caitlin's father didn't pay to have his daughter get lost, either! And the old lady is just lying in bed sleeping. That's just unbelievable," said Michelle

"Michelle, you can really be a brat! How do you think Carlotta feels? Do you think that she's glad that Caitlin ran away? It isn't her fault!" responded Amy.

"Then why isn't she here doing everything in her power to get Caitlin back? I think that's really awful!" retorted Michelle.

Cathy, Kevin, and Cheryl looked at each other for a long time, each sensing the others' growing anger.

What should they do now? Should they say that Carlotta went out searching in the snowstorm? Or should they do as

100

she asked and not say anything? But they couldn't just let Michelle's words stand, could they?

"Hello, my dears. Please clear away your paints and brushes and paper and turn the kitchen over to me and my assistants so that we can perform our culinary dinner magic!" Kevin's mother had arrived in the nick of time. "Where is my team?"

Kieran and Patrick raised their hands, grinning. "Reporting for duty!"

"Oh, two men! How wonderful," said Mrs. Thomas. "So, my dears, I'm going to introduce you to the art of making perfect potato salad and hamburgers today. And what a treat for me – I love cooking with men!"

Kieran rolled his eyes but Patrick clapped his hands.

"I know how to make hamburgers! I've already made them with my mother," he said proudly.

"Terrific! Then let's get started. Kieran, please go get two bags of potatoes out of the pantry, and Patrick can put some water on to boil. Here we go!"

Hal and the others had cleared the table and put the art supplies into a box. Now they were taking the nameplates off the table.

"I think we should get out of here quickly, before they make us help peel the potatoes," he grinned, and led the kids out of the kitchen. He was planning to organize a quiz about horses in the living room, and Kevin, Lena, and Frankie were going to get started on the stable work.

"Hey, I'll help you!" Bev joined the group headed toward the stable. "After all, Lillian isn't back yet."

"Great! Thanks!" Kevin put on his quilted jacket, which had finally dried, and was glad that he could escape into the stalls. Michelle was driving him crazy with her impudent statements and questions.

I feel sorry for Cathy and Cheryl, he thought as the connecting door to the stable shut behind him. He glanced at his watch. In a quarter of an hour, he would try to reach Mr. Lisser again. He had to come home sometime.

Chapter 7

"Can you recognize anything? I'm as blind as a bat!"
Lillian strained to see where they were, but now that it was
getting dark it was impossible to see anything through the
heavy snowfall.

Ricki just shook her head. She was chilled to the bone,
and all she wanted was a hot bath and her bed.

Carlotta held on to Caitlin, who was more hanging than
sitting up in the saddle, as she guided Cora with one hand
and long reins. "We should be home in a few minutes," she
said in a firm voice.

"Are you sure? I can't feel anything anymore.
Everything is numb."

"I'm SURE!"

They rode on in silence, and after a short while a beam
of light appeared in the darkness.

"There it is!" Ricki stared up at the lighted windows of
Mercy Ranch, not too far off.

Carlotta sighed with relief. "Well, girls, we've almost
made it! Cora has brought us safely back home."

Lillian and Ricki looked at each other. "Cora?" Lillian asked.

Carlotta nodded. "Of course, Cora. Who else? Do you think I could see any better than you could? I just relied on my old girl here to find her way back to her warm stall, and she didn't disappoint me."

Ricki remembered that Diablo had once brought her back home at night in a dense fog, and she felt tremendous admiration for a horse's instincts.

"But what would have happened if she hadn't found the trail?" asked Lillian, shivering.

"But she did find it. Nothing else matters."

*

The riders soon reached the ranch and they reined in the animals directly in front of the well-lit stable.

"Ricki, quick! Go in and find someone who can help us lift Caitlin down from the saddle. She needs to get inside immediately!" commanded Carlotta, but before the girl could dismount the stable door flew open and Kevin, Bev, and Lena came running out.

"You're back! Thank goodness! Did you –?"

"Come on, come over here! Caitlin is chilled to the bone. You'll have to be very careful with her. One of you should hold her right side, the other her left, and then ease her down slowly. Lena, you take her legs. Hurry, please!"

Frankie was standing in the stable doorway, looking as pale as a ghost.

"Frankie, open the front door!" Carlotta called to him. "Hurry! Lillian, take Cora into the stable!"

Scared, the ten-year-old jumped at Carlotta's command, but then ran across the hallway and into the house, where he almost collided with Michelle, who was coming back from the bathroom.

"Watch where you're going!"

"Sorry, it's an emergency!" replied the boy, and he headed for the front door.

"Hey, are you crazy?" asked Michelle as Frankie grabbed the doorknob and opened the front door, letting the ice-cold winter air flow into the house. "You're out of your mind! Shut the door right now!"

"They're back! And they found Caitlin!"

"Really?"

"Frankie, open the door a little wider! Quick!" Carlotta's firm voice could be heard, and right afterward, Bev and Kevin came into the house. Between them they barely managed to hold Caitlin in a more or less upright position.

Without worrying about the wet snow she was tracking in, Carlotta hurried past the kids, pushed Michelle brusquely out of the way, and opened the door to the living room.

"Put her down on the couch! Make room!" With a hand gesture, she shooed Amy, Cathy, and Cheryl off the couch, and pushed the coffee table aside.

"What's wrong –?" began Hal, but he stopped talking immediately when he saw that Carlotta was soaking wet and Bev and Kevin were leading Caitlin to the couch.

Quickly, Carlotta took off her jacket and threw it on the floor. "Cathy and Cheryl, you two stay here and help me, the rest of you, out!"

"But –!"

"OUT, I said!" From the tone of Carlotta's voice the kids understood that there was to be no arguing with her and they did as she ordered.

"Oh, Kevin, were you able to reach Mr. Lisser?"

The boy turned in the doorway. "Oh, sorry! I completely forgot to tell you. I did reach him, and he's on his way."

"That's good! Thanks, Kevin! And now, leave us alone here!"

The door had barely closed when Carlotta began to undress the girl.

"Cathy, run up to Caitlin's room right away and get some dry clothes for her to put on. But before you do that, bring me one of those large bath towels, and tell Kevin's mother to fill a hot-water bottle. Cheryl, you'll have to help me. Let's sit her up, and then you can support her while I take off her wet clothes."

"Okay!"

Both girls did as Carlotta ordered, and while Cathy rushed out, Cheryl tried to help Carlotta with her task. She kept looking at Caitlin, who just stared straight ahead at the wall with glassy eyes.

"Can she hear what you say to her?" she asked Carlotta quietly. Carlotta spoke softly and comfortingly to the girl. "She looks like she's seen a ghost!"

At that moment a tired smile spread over Caitlin's face.

"Mama... how nice... I'm... coming... " Weak, she tried to stretch out her arms.

"I have to call the doctor immediately!" whispered Carlotta as she placed a thick fleece blanket over the girl. "Heavens, what's taking Cathy so long?"

"Here I am!" Cathy said, rushing in, and Carlotta began to rub Caitlin's skin until it turned pink.

"Keep going!" she told Cheryl. "I'll be right back!" Carlotta hurried out and disappeared behind the door to her office.

Without taking the time to sit down, she grabbed the phone and dialed the number for the local doctor.

*

Kevin had rushed back to the stable with Bev and Lena to take over the care of the soaking-wet horses from Ricki and Lillian.

"Wow, you two are frozen. Go put on some dry clothes. We'll handle this." Bev pushed Lillian out of Holli's stall and began to unsaddle him.

"Bev's right," Kevin nodded seriously to Ricki, and she could tell by the expression on his face that he had been really worried about her.

"She was lying in the woods when we found her. Lillian spotted her scarf hanging from a tree branch just as we were about to turn back," Ricki began, her teeth chattering, but Kevin shook his head firmly.

"You can tell us all about it later. Go inside and get warm. We'll take care of the horses."

"Okay."

After Ricki and Lillian had disappeared through the connecting door, Lena slid into Diablo's stall.

"If it's okay with you, I'll take him," she said without looking at Ricki's boyfriend.

"Okay! I'll take care of Cora," replied Kevin as he disappeared into the old mare's stall.

"Did you two know that Carlotta was out riding, too?" asked Lena as she dried and groomed Diablo's coat with a brush and a towel.

"Yeah. But she had forbidden us to tell anyone. She didn't want the others to be worried."

"Oh!" Lena shook her head. "That Caitlin is an idiot! Why did she have to run away in such awful weather?"

"Maybe she'll tell you when she's able to," Bev commented from Holli's stall.

"You don't believe that, do you?"

"No, not really. How are you two doing? This white horse is almost dry. I can't do anymore."

"I'm finished with Cora, too, how about you, Lena?"

The girl felt Diablo's coat, and it was hardly damp.

"Oh, I've got some more to do! His belly is still really wet!" she lied.

"Okay, then you can keep going. We already finished with the stable work. I want to go in and check on Ricki. Bev, do you want to stay here or come with me?"

The girl nodded. "I'll come with you. I want to find out how Caitlin is."

"I'm almost finished, and then I'll come in!" Lena continued to brush Diablo's coat and she didn't stop until she heard the connecting door click shut.

"You are such a wonderful animal," she whispered quietly to the black horse, looking at him longingly. He had buried his muzzle in the sweet-smelling hay contentedly. "Why couldn't you belong to me?"

The desire to ride Diablo grew within Lena, and the more she wanted to ride him, the less she liked Ricki, who was never going to allow that to happen. Lena shut her eyes for a moment and imagined herself astride the black horse and flying across the wintry landscape.

"And I am going to ride you!" she said out loud, without realizing it.

"You wouldn't dare! Ricki would kill you!"

Lena turned around and stared in amazement at Michelle, who was standing in the stable.

"Where did you come from? Do you always creep up on people like that?"

Michelle grinned. "I didn't creep up, but people who are so lost in their thoughts, like you, don't hear much."

"What are you doing here? Aren't you supposed to be with the others?" asked Lena angrily, and she hurried out of Diablo's stall.

"I could ask you the same thing," replied Michelle.

"We just took care of the animals, you can see that!"

"Who's we? The only one I see is you, and I heard what you said!"

"You can't have heard anything, because I didn't say anything!" Lena wanted to go back to the house, but she stopped when Michelle spoke to her again.

"I don't know what you find so wonderful about Diablo. I like Sharazan a lot better. It must be amazing to ride him."

"Why don't you just ask Kevin if he'll let you ride him?"

Michelle made a face. "You're not going to ask either, are you?"

"What?"

"Well, if you can ride Diablo?"

"I have, well, more or less, but Ricki –"

"She's a jerk!" Michelle blurted out.

"Are you serious?"

"Yeah! Everybody says she's so great, just because she found Caitlin."

"But Lillian was there too, and Carlotta –"

"Well, apparently Lillian wanted to turn back earlier, but Ricki insisted that they keep looking, and Carlotta didn't

109

get there until the two of them had already found Caitlin. So it's thanks to Ricki that that girl is back."

"Terrific! The woman of the hour!" Lena's voice dripped with sarcasm.

"Something like that."

For a moment the two of them were silent, and they just stared at each other, trying to guess what the other was thinking.

"You don't like her at all, do you?" Michelle asked.

"No!" Lena's answer came back sharp and abrupt. "Ever since Mercy Ranch opened, Bev, Hal, Kieran, Cheryl, and I have been coming every day, helping Carlotta where we could, and it was a lot of fun. But as soon as Ricki and her friends showed up, I felt as though we became unimportant. It's been like that for weeks. And I'm tired of it!" Lena turned her gaze to the side so that Michelle couldn't see that she was lying. After all, until yesterday morning, she hadn't even known that Ricki and Diablo existed, but the girl had the feeling that Michelle could become her ally.

"Really? So bad?"

"Worse." Lena's gaze came back to Diablo.

"She promised that I could ride him, but every time I ask her about it she doesn't want to talk about it. That's really mean, isn't it? I mean, if she doesn't want anyone to ride Diablo, then she shouldn't have promised me in the first place. I'm really mad at her."

"I can understand that," Michelle nodded. That's exactly how she had imagined Ricki. "And now you still want to ride him?"

Lena hesitated for a fraction of a second before she answered, "Yeah! As long as she doesn't find out!"

Michelle grinned. "Don't worry. She won't hear anything from me! You're really cool! But how are you going to do it? I mean, she watches over that horse with eagle eyes."

Lena bit her lips and thought it over. "Well, if you really don't tell on me, then –"

"I'll be as silent as the grave!" Michelle interrupted her new friend in mid-sentence.

"Okay, then listen up. I just thought of something. We could –"

"We?"

"Well, maybe you'd like to come with me. I thought you wanted to ride Sharazan." Lena knew she could be certain that Michelle wouldn't tell on her only if she could make her a co-conspirator.

Michelle looked doubtfully at her. Even though there was nothing she would have liked better than to ride around a ring on Sharazan, she wasn't so sure that she had the guts to ride the animal behind Kevin's back.

"I'm not sure."

Lena looked at her with contempt. "What's with you? First you say you will, and then you're too scared to do it. I didn't think you were like that."

"I'm not. Okay! I'll come with you."

Lena grinned at her new accomplice. "Are you sure?"

"Yeah!"

"Okay. I thought we could –"

*

Caitlin lay on her bed wrapped warmly in a thick comforter. Carlotta and Ricki sat with her and tried to get her to eat some hot broth while they waited for the doctor.

"Come on, eat something. You have to get your strength back. Your father is on his way," said Carlotta with a smile.

"I don't like it," Caitlin answered weakly, but she did open her mouth.

"That doesn't matter! Eat it anyway! It's good for you and it will make you feel better. We don't want your father to be even more worried about you, do we?"

Caitlin sighed. "He's going to kill me!"

Carlotta laughed softly. "I doubt that. At least, he was very relieved to hear that we found you. Don't worry, Caitlin, it's going to be okay."

After a few spoonfuls, the girl suddenly looked at Ricki, who was watching her silently.

"My mother was with me," she said softly.

Ricki was startled.

"She was surrounded by a wonderful light. I never saw her like that before," Caitlin continued. "Suddenly, coming out of nowhere, she was there and she spoke to me! She said that I shouldn't run away from life, and that I shouldn't be sad because she's no longer with me. And she said that Dad really loves me and that I should be happy again."

Carlotta looked straight at the girl, and it was obvious what was going through her mind.

Ricki felt a shiver going down her spine, listening to Caitlin's words.

"You were chilled to the bone, my child, and you weren't really thinking straight when we found you. I'm sure it was a dream, that you –"

Caitlin shook her head.

"I saw her, Carlotta! I swear to you! She said that I shouldn't be afraid, and that everything was going to be all right. She... she walked beside your horse when you brought me home, and she was standing in your living room, too. I'm not crazy! You have to believe me!" Caitlin's eyes filled with tears.

"You're not crazy, sweetie, but I think that you simply wished for your mother to come back to you at that moment, and that's why you saw her."

Caitlin sighed painfully. "Maybe... maybe that's what happened, I don't know," she admitted, but at the moment she was too exhausted to think about it.

*

Michelle and Lena came into the kitchen together, the best of friends. The others were already sitting around the big oval table, and Kevin's mother was filling one plate after another with potato salad and hamburgers.

"You got here just in time," she said and smiled at the two girls. "Sit down. Kieran and Patrick are fantastic cooks. You'll love it."

Michelle glanced at the two boys, who were enjoying the praise, and sneered.

"If that's true, then they might as well do kitchen duty for the rest of the week," she suggested.

Kieran turned up his nose in annoyance. "Definitely not! Once is okay, but seven days? No way. I think I'd rather run away!"

"Run away? So now you're trying to compete with Caitlin?"

"That's ridiculous! And, by the way, I didn't think that was funny!"

113

"Well, as far as I'm concerned, she's not all there. She says that she saw her mother in a bright light! How nuts is that?!" Hal shook his head in disbelief.

"A ghost? Really?" Amy turned pale. "How do you know that?"

"I heard her, a while ago, when I was walking past her room. She told Carlotta."

"This place is haunted. Cool!" laughed Patrick, but he got a nasty look from Lillian. "Why are you looking at me like that? After all, mothers don't usually watch over their daughter's riding vacations in the form of bright lights, do they?"

Lillian poked around in her potato salad. She was exhausted from the search in the cold, and the conversation was getting on her nerves.

"You guys should stop making fun of Caitlin and her mother. You haven't forgotten that she's dead, have you?"

"Oh, come on, take it easy! I didn't mean it like that, but I just think what Caitlin said about her mother appearing to her is the dumbest thing I ever heard!" Hal tried to defend himself.

"Hey, Pat, these hamburgers are really good! I'll have to tell Mom that you're going to take over the cooking from now on." Karen gave him the thumbs up.

"You guys haven't even mentioned the salad!" Kieran pretended to pout.

"Well, honestly," Bev started, "too much salt, too much vinegar, too many spices, too –"

"One more word, Lady Bev, and I'll turn into a wild animal!" Kieran warned his riding companion, who winked at him.

"As long as you turn into a wild horse, I don't care," she said. "In that case, we could break you and you could stay here at the ranch when you get old."

114

"That's perfect, 'cause then you'd have to clean out my stall! I –" Kieran hadn't finished what he was saying when the doorbell started to ring, and kept on going nonstop.

"Who could that be at this time of night?" asked Frankie, his mouth full.

"I have no idea, but we'll soon find out," answered Kevin's mother. She wiped her hands on her apron and left the kitchen to open the door, but Kevin beat her to it.

"I'll get the door, Mom. That's either Caitlin's father or the doctor," he explained quickly as he walked past his mother. Not two minutes later, he was taking Mr. Lisser to Caitlin's room.

Carlotta started to welcome him, but the man just gazed at her with a worried look, before he sank to his knees in front of his daughter's bed.

"Why?" he whispered hoarsely, while his slightly trembling hand wrapped itself around her hand and gently pressed it.

"I'm so sorry, Daddy," replied Caitlin in a soft hesitant voice. Tears flowed over her reddened cheeks.

"Why did you do it? Why did you run away? Don't you know how much you scared us all? And I thought, when I left, that everything was okay with you, but you – Don't you understand how much trouble you could have caused Mrs. Mancini?"

"That's not so important anymore," Carlotta tried to smooth everything over. "The main thing is that she's back, and that no one was hurt."

"I'm so sorry," the girl repeated, sobbing. "I didn't want to come here, and I had the feeling that you were trying to get rid of me because I was becoming just too much for you. After all, you always said that it just couldn't go on like that anymore, and that you didn't know what to do with me."

John Lisser closed his eyes in despair. "You know I never meant it like that, Linnie dear. I just didn't know what to do to get you out of your depression. Before your mother died, you were always so full of life, always doing things, and so happy. And now, it seems you've lost all the joy and happiness you had, and I don't know what I can do to ease your heartache. It makes me crazy to see how you shut yourself off from everything, and I really thought that here, with the horses, you could regain your joy of living. I never wanted to be rid of you, do you hear me? Never! You're the only thing that's left for me from our once-happy family. How could you think that?"

"She was there!" whispered Caitlin, who was terribly upset that she had caused her father to worry so much.

John Lisser listened carefully. "You saw her? When?" he asked, his heart beating wildly.

"When I was lying in the woods. She was wrapped in a bright shining light."

Carlotta and Ricki exchanged a quick glance.

"She said that she saw her mother outside, and also on the way back, and even here in the living room," Ricki said.

Carlotta's voice sounded a little hoarse. "I think perhaps it was a dream caused by her fever, or a wish."

Mr. Lisser turned back to his daughter. "Did you see her or feel her?" he asked.

Caitlin closed her eyes and shrugged her shoulders. "I... I think I saw her, but... I had the feeling that she was very close to me... holding me in her arms!"

116

That was Carlotta and me, thought Ricki, and she felt really sorry for Caitlin. She must have really loved her mother if she had escaped into this fantasy.

John got up. "Well, I've never spoken about it, but... I feel the presence of my wife too sometimes. It's a feeling I can't describe, and I wonder, seriously, if maybe it's possible after all, to see a person who has died... well, the soul, I mean."

Carlotta looked in disbelief at Caitlin and her father, and thought that they must be grieving very deeply to have created these images and feelings.

"I know what you think, Mrs. Mancini," said John Lisser softly. "But we're not crazy. I'm convinced that there are things that our brains cannot understand that exist nevertheless."

Ricki felt a shiver go down her spine. She had read somewhere that there were people who believed they could sense or see dead people, but she had never actually believed these stories, at least not until now.

"I'm going to go downstairs and join the others," she stammered, and left quickly. She needed to leave the room, which seemed to be pressing in on her. She had to go outside, into the fresh air. What she had heard frightened her, but it also fascinated her.

She was already on her way to the front door when she changed her mind and ran back. Diablo was the only one who could help her calm down.

*

About ten minutes later, the doctor arrived at the ranch. After examining Caitlin, he announced that the girl had

117

gotten chilled but that there wasn't anything seriously wrong with her. However, just to be on the safe side, he insisted that she be admitted to the hospital for a day or two, for observation.

Regretfully, Carlotta said good-bye to Caitlin and promised her that she could come back anytime.

"Take care, child, and good luck" she said softly as she stood in the doorway and watched the cars slowly disappear into the darkness.

Chapter 8

Two days went by, during which the kids could think and talk about little else besides Caitlin and her misadventure. But daily life returned to normal after John Lisser returned to the ranch and reported that his daughter had recuperated much faster than he had even dared to hope.

"She asked me to say hello to everyone for her and to apologize for giving you all such a hard time. She especially wanted to thank you, Mrs. Mancini, and also Ricki, for everything you did for her. Caitlin would like to come back in the summer, if that's all right with you. Oh, by the way, my daughter and I had a long talk, and we have decided to move on with our lives and try to be a happy family again," he explained, a little embarrassed, before he said good-bye.

That's one less worry, thought Carlotta with relief. Now she could concentrate on the rest of her guests, whose days were to be filled with chores connected with horse care, games, kitchen duty, boisterous snowball fights, and, of course, riding.

As soon as the snowfall stopped, and the sun transformed the wintry fields into a magical landscape, the kids were finally allowed to saddle their horses and ride locally, under the watchful eyes of Ricki and her friends.

Frankie, Patrick, Amy, and Karen sat tall and proud on their favorite horses, which were led on ropes by the older riders.

"I feel more comfortable with this," Carlotta had said, when the ten-year-olds at first protested this arrangement. Eventually they came to admit that they didn't know enough about riding to go off in the countryside alone.

"Well, I don't care! I know that I don't ride very well yet. I just erase the lead rope in my head," laughed Frankie and he patted Silver's neck proudly. "When I come back next year, I'm sure I'll be ready to ride on my own."

"Are you really going to come back here?" asked Patrick.

"Of course! I love it here."

"Well, then, I'll get my mother to let me come back again, too."

Frankie nodded enthusiastically. "That would be awesome!"

*

After lunch, Carlotta surprised her guests by inviting them to go to the movies.

"There's a film about the life of a race horse that I thought might appeal to you," she announced with a broad smile, and the kids broke out in loud cheering.

"All, right! Yeah! I saw the previews! The movie's supposed to be fantastic!" Cheryl's eyes lit up happily.

"We could go somewhere afterward and get a bite to eat, and that would mean that kitchen duty is canceled for today."

"Hooray!" Amy and Ricki grinned at each other.

"What luck," laughed Ricki, and she leaned back, relaxed.

"Typical!" whispered Lena to Michelle. "What else is new? Of course, on the day that Ricki has kitchen duty, we're going to the movies and out to eat! That is really unbelievable!"

"But we do have one small problem," continued Carlotta.

"And what would that be?" asked Kieran, and the others listened intently as well. They couldn't imagine how going to the movies could be a problem.

"Well, I don't want to go to the evening show. The streets will be icy later on tonight, and neither I, nor Kevin's mother, who has to drive as well, want to take any risks with you in the cars. That's why we're going to the afternoon show."

"And what's the problem?" asked Kieran, who didn't care when he saw the movie.

"Well, we have to leave a little before three o'clock, and we won't be back until about seven-thirty. That means that the horses will be on their own and that we won't be here to feed them. Honestly, that's the one thing that is really bothering me. It's important to me to keep the horses on schedule."

Lena saw her chance.

"I... well, I've already seen the movie! I can stay here and take care of the horses. I don't mind at all," she said quickly and with emphasis, and looked at Michelle entreatingly. "Maybe you could bring me back some French fries."

"I'll stay here, too," said Ricki spontaneously. Diablo was much more important to her than any film about racehorses. "Between the two of us, we'll get the chores in the stall done easily. What do you say, Lena?"

Carlotta smiled happily. She had known that she could rely on her crew.

Oh, no, that wasn't the way Lena had imagined it. Her mind worked feverishly. Good grief, that Michelle is really an idiot! Didn't she realize that this afternoon would be the chance of a lifetime to go riding secretly?

"Good, then let's say everybody will be dressed and ready just before three o'clock, so we can leave on time. I think it's really great of Lena and Ricki to take on the stable chores, and we'll bring them back a meal fit for a king!" Carlotta nodded approvingly at them, and then she left to discuss the trip with Kevin's mother.

"Should I stay, too, and help you?" asked Kevin as he put his arm around Ricki.

"No, no. Go with them. I know you want to see the movie."

"But I could stay here and then we could go together when we get back home."

Ricki shook her head and laughed. "Take advantage of the fact that Carlotta's paying," she grinned at her boyfriend before she turned to Lena.

"We'll get through these few hours, won't we?" she winked at Lena, who forced herself to smile back innocently.

"There's nothing else we can do," grumbled Lena, before she took Michelle's arm and jerked her toward the door. "Would you please come with me for a minute? I want to show you something!"

"Really? What?" Michelle looked at her puzzled.

"It's a secret! Come on!"

Lena pulled her friend upstairs and into her room and closed the door behind them.

"What do you want to show me?" asked Michelle again, but Lena just shook her head.

"Nothing. I just want to talk with you."

"What about?"

Lena rolled her eyes. "What do you think? Michelle, you're really dense. Why didn't you volunteer to help with the stable chores? When the others are all gone, that would have been our chance to go riding!"

Michelle slapped her forehead with her hand. "Duh! I didn't even think of that!"

"Yeah, I noticed."

"What now?"

"We'll never have a better chance! If you really want to ride Sharazan, then go to Ricki and tell her that you'll take over her chores so that she can see the movie with Kevin."

Michelle hesitated. "Of course I would like to ride Sharazan, but maybe it would be better to ask Kevin, instead of –"

Lena looked at her contemptuously. "That's what I thought. You talk big, but when push comes to shove, you chicken out! You're really a loser, Michelle."

"I'm not a loser!"

"Yes you are, a coward and a loser." Lena turned to go. She knew that she would be in big trouble if Michelle told on her, but she could still deny everything, and then she'd find out who Carlotta would believe more, a guest at the ranch or a reliable ranch hand who had helped out in the stable every day.

"Okay." she heard Michelle's voice, very quiet.

"What?"

"I said okay. I'll do it!" Michelle took a deep breath. She was uncomfortable with the thought that she was about to go behind the backs of all the people here who had been so friendly to her, but then again, she didn't want Lena to think that she was a coward.

"I'll believe that when I see it!" Lena opened the door and pointed outside. "Well, get going!"

Michelle nodded obediently. What had she gotten herself into?

*

At first, Ricki had been skeptical when Michelle had offered to take her place and stay at the ranch with Lena. But when Carlotta said she didn't mind, since Lena had been helping with the horses for weeks, she was glad to have the chance to see the movie with Kevin after all.

They stood together with the others around the cars and heard Carlotta give Lena the final instructions.

"And make sure that the stall doors are really closed, so that Hadrian and Silver don't get out and start wandering around on their own. You know that the clasps stick a little. And don't give the ponies too much hay! Sometimes you forget that they aren't as big as the horses, and sometimes, when I see those filled racks –"

Lena smiled her sweetest smile.

"Don't worry, Carlotta, we'll take care of everything! When you come back, they'll all be standing in their stalls munching on their hay and waiting for you to tell them all about the world of racehorses," she laughed, and no one noticed that it sounded a little false.

"Okay. Then let's get going!" Carlotta turned to the other kids, who were getting impatient. "Everyone into the cars. We're leaving!"

Michelle went over to stand next to Lena, and together they watched the others leave.

When the sound of the cars could no longer be heard, Lena breathed a sigh of relief.

"Good! We're finally rid of them!" she said and rushed into the stable, with Michelle right behind her. "If we go riding right away, there'll be enough time afterward to get the horses' coats groomed, and no one will see that they've been ridden. We have about an hour, then we have to be back here if we want to be finished with the stable chores in time. There are a few stalls that need to be swept out."

Michelle's heart was beating wildly as Lena pushed her into the tack room and showed her Sharazan's saddle.

"We won't brush the horses much now, or we'll lose too much time. They were brushed this morning, anyway," Lena said. "Let's go! We'll saddle up and then leave." Determined, she grabbed Diablo's saddle and snaffle and then marched straight to the black horse's stall.

"Hey, you," said Lena tenderly. "Let's see if you're as great to ride as everyone says."

"Lena," Michelle began, "I know this may sound stupid, but I have a really bad feeling about this."

"Are you going to start whining again? Come on! This will be a fabulous ride! Just imagine galloping along the snow-covered meadow on this magnificent roan, while his mane whips back in your face! You'll never forget it, and Sharazan probably won't either!"

Michelle took a deep breath, and then, with trembling hands, she opened the gate to Sharazan's stall. The image that Lena's words had conjured in her mind was irresistible. She saddled the gelding quickly, while Lena got Diablo

125

ready for the ride, and together they led the animals out of the stable.

"Here we go!" exclaimed Lena excitedly, and she pulled Diablo after her. The black horse laid his ears back a little. There was nothing he hated more than the pressure of the bit in his mouth when the reins were pulled.

"Come on, you beauty! We have to hurry before Ricki gets back, or there's going to be a huge fight!"

*

Not five minutes later, the two girls sat in the saddles of two horses they weren't used to riding and let them trot along the path with loose reins.

In the beginning, Michelle sat stiffly in the saddle, but with every step that Sharazan took away from the ranch, she felt more and more at ease, and after a short time she began to enjoy her ride on her dream horse.

"Didn't I tell you it would be great?" Lena called to her over her shoulder. "How about a gallop?"

"Yeah!" replied Michelle, her eyes shining brightly, and pretty soon she completely forgot that they didn't have permission to ride these horses.

"Yeah!" Lena pressed her thighs against Diablo's body and the black horse shot off like a rocket. Sharazan didn't even wait for his rider to urge him, but just raced after his stall companion with wide reaching steps.

Michelle had never ridden at such a fast gallop in her life, and she got frightened when she noticed that the roan had begun to skid in a few icy places.

"Lena," she yelled over the flowing mane, "Lena, slow down! It's too icy here! Lena –"

Diablo's rider heard Michelle calling, but she just let Ricki's horse run faster and faster.

This is incredible, she kept thinking. *What a dream ride!*

"Lena!" Michelle pulled hard on the reins, desperately trying to stop the horse.

Michelle's horrified scream seemed to awaken Lena from a dream, and she reined in Diablo until the black horse stood still, breathing hard, with thick clouds of hot air around his muzzle.

"Are you crazy, going that fast?" Michelle trembled a little, as Sharazan finally stood still, too. "He doesn't have any shoes! I thought a couple of times that we were going to fall, he was sliding so much!"

"Really?" Lena grinned. "I didn't even notice that it was slippery!"

"Oh, I forgot! Diablo has calkins," said Michelle.

"Of course! Why do you think I was able to let him run?"

Michelle breathed out angrily. "You wouldn't have cared if I'd fallen, would you? At least you had fun!"

"Oh, come on, don't make such a big deal out of this! You're having fun, too, admit it, and anyway, nothing happened!"

"No, up till now, nothing, but if you're going to ride around like a crazy person, something might!"

"Okay, okay! You're right. It was stupid of me," responded Lena, and with that she and Michelle were friends again. "Come on, I'll show you Echo Lake. It's beautiful when it's frozen over."

"There's a lake around here? I didn't know that."

"There's a lot you don't know yet," laughed Lena and patted Diablo's sweaty neck as she guided him into the woods.

127

"Well, that just can't be, can it?" Carlotta stood in front of the movie theater, which was closed, with her bunch of kids. "Didn't anyone remember that today is Tuesday and there's no afternoon matinee?"

The kids, whose disappointment was obvious on their faces at first, started to giggle, one after the other.

"Nope, Carlotta! We thought you'd booked a special matinee just for us!" laughed Kevin and pulled Ricki closer.

"Exactly! We'd never have guessed that you wanted us to watch the film with the regular moviegoers!" grinned Kieran.

Now Carlotta had to laugh. "Well, there's nothing we can do about it now. It's my fault. I should have looked at the schedule more closely. You know what? Then we'll just go to plan two of the day. The only question is: Do we bring Michelle and Lena cake, or hamburgers and French fries?"

"Both!"

Sighing, Carlotta resigned herself to her fate. "Okay, but only because I messed up with the movie."

"There are good and bad sides to everything," announced Hal, winking at Bev, who was shivering and holding onto his arm.

"Then let's go!" ordered Carlotta. "And as an 'I'm sorry,' gesture, we'll start with dessert first."

"Hurray!' twelve voices shouted in unison.

Ten minutes later, they entered the café and each of them picked out a dessert at the buffet.

"I wonder if Lena and Michelle are doing okay at the stable?" Ricki asked suddenly, and for a moment there was silence at the table.

"Why wouldn't they?" Kevin asked.

"No reason. I just wondered."

"Oh, I thought you were having another one of your premonitions," grinned Lillian at her girlfriend.

Ricki stared at her. "Premonitions?" she said. "I don't know –"

"Don't tell me you can predict things," teased Bev, who didn't know Ricki that well yet. She didn't know that Ricki could often sense when something dangerous was happening or about to happen nearby.

"Not really," replied Ricki quietly. But she kept moving restlessly back and forth in her chair, constantly looking at her watch. Time seemed to stand still. Her thoughts were on Diablo, and she couldn't shake the feeling that she'd rather be with him than here in the café, even though the atmosphere was great.

Something's wrong, thought Ricki nervously, and she glanced over at Carlotta, who gave no sign that she was ready to leave.

Carlotta was talking to Kevin's mother about whether or not it would make more sense for her and Kevin to move to Carlotta's ranch, since she spent most of her time there anyway, taking care of Carlotta's household.

"Wow, did you hear that, Ricki? If Mom accepts Carlotta's offer, then I'll become a permanent resident at the ranch too. Cool, isn't it?" Kevin's eyes began to shine. "Ricki, did you hear what I said?"

"What did you say?" she asked, bewildered.

"I said that Mom and I might move to the ranch soon. What's with you?" Concerned, Kevin stared into the tense face of his girlfriend.

"Oh, do you think you'll let Sharazan stay in our stalls, or will you take him with you?"

"I haven't thought about it yet," Kevin admitted. The idea that he wouldn't have to ride his bike for miles just to ride his horse appealed to him, but on the other hand, he hated to take Sharazan away from his familiar surroundings and from his horse friends. And the thought that he wouldn't see Ricki every day didn't exactly appeal to him either.

"Probably stay," he replied, but Ricki didn't hear him. Her thoughts were still focused on Diablo. From their first day together, Ricki and Diablo had forged a very close relationship, and every time the black horse was in trouble, Ricki sensed it immediately.

"I shouldn't have come," she said softly to herself, and was relieved when Carlotta waved to the waitress and asked for the bill.

"So, now you really want to eat some hamburgers?" she asked, as she got up a little awkwardly.

"Of course!" answered Kieran. "You have no idea how much I can fit into this stomach!"

"Oh, no!" groaned Ricki. Since they had eaten dessert first she had completely forgotten about lunch. She racked her brain, trying to think of something to convince the others to return to the ranch right away. Frantically, she glanced at her watch. If they left now, they would be home soon.

"Say, how would it be if we just stopped and got take out," suggested Carlotta, suddenly. "I think Lena and Michelle wouldn't mind if we helped them with the stable chores."

"Great idea!" Ricki burst out loudly.

Carlotta turned to her and looked Ricki straight in the eye. She knew her well enough to know that there was something more behind the quick answer than just a desire to be with Diablo.

She motioned for Ricki to come closer.

"What's wrong?" she asked quietly, and the girl shrugged her shoulders.

"I don't know exactly, but something's wrong. I can't explain it," whispered Ricki, pale as a ghost.

"You have that funny feeling again, don't you?"

Ricki nodded slowly and lowered her head.

Carlotta's expression turned serious. She had learned to trust Ricki's intuition. She gave her a long look before she put her hand on her shoulder, and then she turned to the other kids.

"People, I just remembered that I forgot to make an important phone call. So let's get our burgers and go home, okay?" Carlotta was convincing.

"Can't you just use your cell phone?" asked Kevin's mother.

"No. I have the number at home, and I'll be in serious trouble if I don't make that call," she continued with her story.

"Okay! This just proves there's a reason for everything, and that's why the theater was closed this afternoon," laughed Cheryl.

"Okay, then let's get going. After all, we can't be responsible for getting Carlotta in trouble," Kevin said gallantly as he helped Ricki into her thick quilted jacket.

"The story about the phone call isn't true, is it?" he whispered to his girlfriend.

131

"No."

"I knew it. You're having one of your funny feelings again, aren't you?"

Ricki nodded and grabbed his hand. "I'm scared, Kevin. I just hope nothing has happened to the horses."

Chapter 9

"This is so beautiful. Echo Lake is an absolute dream. A real fairytale landscape. It must be a wonderful place to visit in the summer." Michelle's eyes began to glisten at the sight of the gleaming frozen surface.

Lena grinned. "Absolutely! Everyone comes here for swimming. You can keep to yourself here, even when there are lots of people lying around the lake catching some rays."

"Have you ever been swimming on horseback? I mean, can you take the horses in, or is that not allowed?"

"I have no idea about that. Mercy Ranch wasn't in operation last summer, so I didn't do any riding. Maybe Ricki and her friends have been here with their horses. Diablo and Sharazan seem to be familiar with the area. At least Sharazan doesn't seem to be afraid of the frozen lake." The roan had gone very close to the ice and was looking at the hard surface, as though he couldn't believe that he couldn't drink out of the lake today. Diablo stayed a little more at a distance.

Michelle laughed. "It's a pretty huge lake! What's that

over there?" she asked, pointing across to the other side. "Is that a hut? I can't tell from here. I forgot to put in my contacts this morning."

"So you're as blind as I am," grinned Lena and straightened her glasses a little. "But you're right. It is a hut. There used to be a boat rental there, but ever since the woods were declared a nature preserve, boats aren't allowed on the lake."

"I love nature preserves," said Michelle. "You feel as though you're in a primitive jungle. Hey, can you ride over there?"

"You can, but that would take too long, because we would have to ride all around the lake." Lena thought about it briefly. "But there is another possibility."

"Really? What?"

Lena pointed at the ice. "We could ride across the lake. The surface is frozen solid."

Michelle swallowed excitedly. "Are you crazy! That's much too dangerous!"

"And you're a coward!"

"I'd rather be a live coward than a dead hero!"

"You'll always be a loser!" Lena said nastily.

"I'm not a loser!"

"Yes, you are! A little cowardly loser!"

"That's not true, but –"

"If you have the guts, show me. Ride across!" Lena raised her finger and pointed across the frozen lake.

"If you're so brave, why don't you ride across?" Michelle's voice shook with a mixture of fear and anger.

"No problem, but you're coming with me." Lena gave Sharazan's rider a challenging look, but secretly she hoped that Michelle wouldn't accept the challenge. It was easy to talk big, but an entirely different story to risk taking the horses onto the ice. Lena was pretty scared herself to risk the dangerous ride, but it was really fun to provoke Michelle.

"So, how about it? Are you coming with me?" she asked, trying to hide her own fears. Meanwhile she stared at Michelle, taunting her.

Michelle closed her eyes. She was torn. Lena had touched a nerve. Her classmates at school considered the twelve-year-old a coward. She never participated in pranks and always withdrew if, for example, the others were diving from the high board into the pool. She hadn't gone along on night walks because the owls screeching in the dark frightened her. Even her little sister was more courageous than she was. If Amy knew what a timid soul her sister was, she would tell the whole school. However, if Michelle could brag about riding across the frozen lake during winter vacation, then the others wouldn't call her a coward anymore. And suddenly she realized why she had agreed to go on this ride.

"Come on!" Lena picked up Diablo's reins and urged him a few steps toward the lake.

She had never imagined that the girl would follow her, and she was startled when she suddenly saw Sharazan's head next to her.

"Good, I'll come with you!" When she heard Michelle's voice her heart skipped a beat.

There's no going back now, she thought, as her stomach cramped in fear. *If I don't go through with this, I'll lose face forever!"*

"Are you sure?" asked Lena, her voice trembling, and Michelle nodded.

"I'm not a coward!"

"Okay!" Lena took a deep breath and guided Diablo carefully onto the ice.

*

"It smells like French fries," Amy announced giggling, as she tried to hold the paper bag high enough so that the grease from the fries didn't stain her clothes.

"They smell wonderful," Frankie said as he shoved a few fries into his mouth.

Ricki, who was sitting in the passenger seat beside Carlotta, stared straight ahead. It seemed to her that the trip was taking forever, but she knew that it was impossible to drive any faster on the icy roads.

"It's getting dark earlier than I thought today," murmured Carlotta. "I'm glad we're on our way home." She glanced quickly at Ricki sitting next to her. "Do you still have that funny feeling?" she asked, worried.

Ricki nodded. The indefinable fear within her was growing steadily. She was relieved when they finally arrived at Mercy Ranch, but the mounting anxiety kept her hands gripped to her seat as Carlotta carefully brought the car to a halt in the ranch driveway.

"Why are the wheelbarrows outside?" whispered Ricki tonelessly. "Shouldn't Lena and Michelle be using them in the stable by now?"

"Maybe they've already finished," Carlotta tried to console the girl, but Ricki had opened the car door and was running across to the stable.

"What's wrong with her? Did she see a ghost, too? Why did she suddenly run off like that?"

"I'll bet she's not feeling well."

"Probably. Either she ate too much cake or Carlotta's driving made her carsick."

"You're bad!" Kevin grinned at the kids, but then he ran after his girlfriend. Carlotta followed as quickly as she could, too, while the others followed Kevin's mother through the door and into the warm house to devour their hamburgers and fries.

*

Ricki stood in the corridor of the stable in total disbelief, incapable of saying anything. She stared numbly at the two stalls in which Diablo and Sharazan had been contentedly munching their hay before they all left for the movie.

Kevin was as pale as his girlfriend, and Carlotta had the feeling that the floor was collapsing under her feet.

"Where are our horses?" breathed Ricki in shock.

"They're gone!" responded Kevin, stating the obvious.

"Just a moment!" Carlotta pushed the two of them aside, glanced into the unswept stalls, and then hobbled over to the tack room as quickly as she could.

"That's what I was afraid of!" she murmured furiously to herself when she saw that Diablo and Sharazan's saddles and snaffles were missing. "When I catch those two, they're going to be in big trouble!" she said harshly, her face bright red. She went back out into the stable's corridor and looked into the worried and questioning faces of Ricki and Kevin.

"It's all my fault!" Carlotta shook with anger. "I thought I could trust Lena, but I was wrong! Instead of taking care of the horses, she must have persuaded Michelle to go riding. I should have known!"

137

"But why Diablo and Sharazan?" asked Ricki, her voice hoarse.

"I wish I knew!"

"Hey, what are you doing? Your food is getting cold!" Lillian and Cathy rushed in, laughing.

"What's going on here? You look like you just lost your best friend."

Ricki pointed silently at the empty stalls.

"Oh, no! Where are Diablo and Sharazan?"

"The two of them are apparently carrying Lena and Michelle around outside!" Carlotta ground her teeth. She was furious with herself.

"Really?"

"Yes, and I don't even know what I'm going to do with them when they get back!"

"If they'd just asked permission first!" Kevin said angrily, then he stomped outside to get one of the wheelbarrows. With a furious bang he put it in front of the first stall and went to get a pitchfork. He couldn't just stand around doing nothing, waiting for Sharazan to get back.

Ricki followed his lead mechanically. Lillian and Cathy had lost their appetites, so they began feeding the horses while the other two cleaned out the stalls.

As Carlotta watched the four friends at work, she chastised herself for being so wrong about Lena. Apparently, the girl didn't have even a fraction of the sense of responsibility that Ricki and her friends demonstrated again and again, every day.

*

The ice cracked threateningly under the hooves of the horses as they left the firm ground of the shore.

Go back, before it's too late, thundered through Lena's mind, but she forced herself not to listen to her inner voice. She would never show Michelle how frightened she was, even if she died a thousand deaths on this ride. She would never admit that it was the stupidest idea of all time to go out on the ice with the horses, especially since the lake wasn't even officially declared safe to walk on.

Michelle was feeling the same.

She was uncontrollably frightened and the fear had transferred itself to Sharazan. Restlessly, the roan began to throw his head up and down, while he began to dance nervously on the slippery surface.

"Easy, Sharazan. Everything's okay!" she tried to control her own fear and calm the horse.

Nothing's okay! something within her screamed. *Why are you taking this risk? Have you completely lost your mind?*

Lena kept swallowing hard. Her heart beat wildly and she had a lump in her throat. She felt as though one thoughtless moment could transform this wonderful idyll of a wintry landscape into a nightmare.

The girl tried to overcome her pride and turn back, when all of a sudden she got a face-saving idea. When she reached the middle of the lake, she would glance at her watch and gesture to Michelle that it was time to ride back so that they could feed the horses before Carlotta got back with the others. She would –

At that moment, a cracking noise filled the air. Michelle screamed. Sharazan was frightened and reared up. He tried to find some sure footing so that he could gallop back to the shore.

Michelle had fallen out of the saddle and landed on her

back on the ice. She slid several feet and then came to a halt and lay still.

Diablo paid no attention to the pressure of his rider's thighs, or to the tugs on the reins, and raced after the roan.

A second crack echoed across the ice, and now the ice began to creak and splinter under the thundering hooves.

Please don't break through the ice, Lena kept chanting. *Please, don't let anything happen! Oh, I'm so afraid!*

Sharazan had managed, with difficulty, to reach the shoreline safely, but there was still about thirty feet between Diablo and firm ground when the ice gave way completely and the horse and rider broke through.

Lena sobbed and screamed loudly. "Help! NO... Diablo... oh —"

The horse tried to rear up in the water to reach the ice rim with his front hooves, but every time he tried his iron hooves shattered the ice like glass.

Lena could see that at least Diablo could stand on the bottom of the lake. The water there was very shallow. If he had broken through farther out, it would have meant the end for this wonderful animal – and for her too – but now he just stood in chest-high water.

The girl slid carefully out of the saddle and hoped with all her might that the ice would be strong enough to carry her weight, and so far so good. Shivering with fright and cold, she stood beside Diablo, whose head reached up to her stomach. Trembling, she stroked his forehead. Then she threw the reins over his head and began to pull.

"Come on, come on, Diablo! You have to get out of the water!" she screamed at him, but the horse just laid his ears back and let the whites of his eyes show. He

140

stretched his neck farther and farther, but he made no effort to move forward.

"Oh no, what am I going to do?" sobbed Lena desperately, as she realized that she couldn't move Diablo even an inch. Finally, she undid the buckles on the bit with trembling hands. There was only one possibility of getting the horse to move forward, and she could only hope that Diablo wouldn't change directions and stop heading for the shore. Frightened, she stood behind the horse, closed her eyes for a fraction of a second, sent a prayer toward heaven, and then slapped the reins sharply against Diablo's croup.

"Come on, come on! Hurry up! Forward, Diablo! Get out of here! GET OUT!" Blinded by her tears, she continued to beat the horse, and the black horse finally tried hard to get away. He kept trying again and again to find some firm footing, but he couldn't. Instead, his hooves splintered the ice, and the animal worked his way step by step forward in his panic. Lena kept yelling and urging him on. The last few feet, where the ice only came up to his legs, he gave a few mighty jumps and, finally, he reached the snow-covered shore.

Lena collapsed and watched the black horse gallop away.

"Oh no, what have I done?" she sobbed. She didn't dare think about what else might happen to the two horses now that they were running loose in the snowy countryside. All of a sudden she bolted upright. Michelle!

Trembling, Lena got up and stared at the twelve-year-old, who was still lying on the ice.

"Michelle? Michelle, are you hurt?" she shouted loudly, but she waited in vain for an answer.

"Oh, no! Please, no!" Lena whispered, frightened, before she stood up, shivering, and ran across the ice carefully, afraid that the frozen surface would give way at any moment.

*

Time passed slowly, and Ricki. Lillian and Kevin went outside again and again to see if there was any sign of the missing horses and riders.

"They should have been back a long time ago, shouldn't they? I mean, they know they were supposed to feed the other animals!" Ricki was getting more and more upset, and Kevin was having problems keeping his cool, too.

"Let's get inside. It's too cold! They won't come back any sooner just because we're out here freezing to death!" exclaimed Lillian, but Ricki's nerves were so frayed that she screamed at her girlfriend louder than she'd intended to.

"That's easy for you to say! Your Holli is fine, right there in the stable!" she yelled back. She had to admit, however, that Lillian was actually right. She reached for Kevin's hand and looked at him desperately. "What if something's happened to them?"

Kevin jumped. Ricki had said exactly what kept going through his mind. Still, he tried to keep his cool so as not to frighten his girlfriend even more.

"What could have happened to them? The two of them know how to ride, and our horses aren't difficult," he said.

"But they don't know Sharazan and Diablo. And anyway, besides us, no one else has ridden them for a long time."

"Ricki, for heaven's sake, stop it! Don't make us more crazy than we already are!"

"But –"

"Come with me." Carlotta waved at them as she emerged from the house. "We're going to get in the car and hope that we find them. They can't have gotten far, and I doubt they've completely forgotten about the stable, even though they are wrapped up in their riding adventure!"

The three of them hurried to Carlotta's car and got in, glad to be doing something – anything – besides waiting.

As the car moved slowly over the creaking snow, Ricki said, "Up to now, we've caused you nothing but trouble, haven't we, Carlotta?"

For a moment, the older woman was silent, but then she smiled at Ricki.

"You haven't caused me any trouble. It's not your fault that your horses were taken. It's all my fault, mine alone. I trusted the wrong person, and now I can only hope that the girls and the horses are okay." She breathed deeply and stared into the fading light of dusk.

"Where are we going?" asked Kevin. "We have no idea where to begin searching. It's like it was with Caitlin, only Lena and Michelle could be much farther away."

"That's a good question." Carlotta thought it over. "Where would you ride if you were in their place?"

"To Echo Lake!" Ricki burst out after a moment's thought.

"That's pretty far away," Kevin said. "I can't imagine, that the two of them –"

"It's not that far. If Lena knows her way around here, then she's familiar with the shortcut past the forest ranger's hut. If they gallop once or twice along the way, they could have gotten to the lake in under half an hour," Ricki contradicted him.

143

"Why Echo Lake?" Carlotta wanted to know. "Why wouldn't they ride in another direction?"

"Because Ricki is incredibly romantic and the lake looks gorgeous in the wintertime," answered Kevin.

"Exactly! And because I would have wanted to show it to Michelle. After all, she doesn't know about the lake," added Ricki.

Carlotta hesitated. Could it be that Lena had had the same idea as Ricki? Was it possible that the two of them had really ridden to the lake? But if it took only half an hour to get there, then the girls should have been back a long time ago. But what if Lena didn't know the shortcut?

"What is that?" called Kevin, pressing his nose against the window. "Oh my gosh, Carlotta, stop the car! It's Sharazan!"

The car started to slide dangerously when the driver braked abruptly, and before it had even come to a stop Kevin had torn the door open and jumped into the snow with a huge leap.

"SHARAZAN!" he called loudly, while he ran in the direction of his horse, which was standing between the trees without a rider. The roan looked attentively at his owner.

"Sharazan, hey, my boy, come here!" Kevin tried to get him to come, keeping his voice calm.

Ricki and Carlotta had gotten out of the car, too.

"Where is Diablo?" whispered Ricki, hoarsely.

"And furthermore, where are Lena and Michelle?" asked Carlotta, her expression angry.

Ricki felt as though her legs were going to give out.

"Why is it always Sharazan and Diablo?" she asked out loud.

144

"Maybe it's because you two have wonderful horses that fascinate everyone," suggested Carlotta, and then she breathed a sigh of relief. "Look! He's got him! Thank goodness!"

Kevin had almost reached his horse when Sharazan finally recognized him and walked toward him. Happy and relieved, the boy grabbed the reins and examined his horse closely. He didn't appear to be injured.

"He's okay!" he called to Ricki and Carlotta, as he led Sharazan by his reins.

"Good, one less worry!" Carlotta nodded at him. "Ride him back home right away!"

"There's nothing I'd rather do," responded Kevin, and then he readjusted the stirrups. "But wouldn't it be better, if I –"

"Go home, Kevin! No detours! Do you understand me?"

The boy nodded obediently. He thought he'd better not argue with Carlotta right now.

"And the two of us are going to keep on searching. Come on, Ricki!"

Carlotta was just getting into the car when Diablo's loud whinny interrupted the quiet evening.

Ricki jumped and twirled around.

Almost in the same spot where Sharazan had been found, the huge black horse now appeared, galloping.

"Diablo," whispered the girl. "Here... come here, my sweet boy, come! Boy am I glad to see you!" Then she realized that her horse had come back without a rider as well. "Oh no, what's happened? Oh, how I wish you could tell me!" Moments later, when she wrapped her arms around her horse's neck and was sobbing in his mane, she automatically reached for his reins, but they weren't there.

"Huh? That's impossible! The reins are gone!" she called over her shoulder. "Completely gone! Unbuckled! What can that mean?" As Diablo walked slowly beside her, she noticed that his legs and his belly were covered in ice crystals, and his coat seemed to have been rubbed off in some places.

"Look at that! Diablo is completely frozen around his belly and legs! What happened?" Ricki couldn't explain it, but Carlotta's expression grew harder.

"Ricki, I think you were right," she said slowly. She was glad that the two of them were looking at their horses and couldn't see her ashen face.

"What do you mean? Right about what?"

"Echo Lake!"

Ricki hesitated, and then all of a sudden she understood.

"You mean the ice... Diablo broke through? Please, don't say that. They can't be so stupid that they would ride out on the frozen lake with our horses, can they?" Ricki began to shake all over at the thought. But it would explain why her horse looked like this.

"I didn't say that." Carlotta tried to calm her down. "Maybe the two of them dismounted and the horses just ran off. Maybe Diablo ran out on the ice by himself."

"Never!" Ricki burst out immediately. "He would never run out onto the lake by himself. Ever since that time we swam out to rescue Lillian and Josh, he doesn't like the lake very much."

"Ride home, you two! I'll drive to the lake!" Carlotta decided.

"But what if something really has happened? You'd need help, and you'd be alone."

"That's true. That would be bad!" Carlotta frowned. She didn't have much time. Lena and Michelle had to be found as quickly as possible.

"I could lead Diablo on a rope," suggested Kevin, who was already in the saddle.

"Yeah, great, and how are you going to do that?" Ricki looked uncertain.

"We can undo one of the straps on the stirrup, and then hook it through the ring on the snaffle. That should be long enough."

"Oh, that's good. Wait! Carlotta, could you hold Diablo for a minute?" and Ricki began to undo the straps on the stirrup. It wasn't easy to release the frozen buckles, but she managed. After she had made sure that the temporary reins wouldn't come undone during the ride home, she handed the leather strap to Kevin.

"Be careful!" she said to her boyfriend, concerned, but Kevin just smiled at her encouragingly.

"Don't worry. I'll bring the two of them back to their stalls safe and sound."

"Ricki, come on! We have to get going." Carlotta urged the girl toward the car. "We can't afford to lose any more time!"

*

Lena had reached Michelle, who was lying still on the ice, and she sank down on her knees.

"Oh, Michelle, I'm so sorry! You have to believe me! Michelle, say something! Are you hurt?"

At last, the twelve-year-old raised her head and stared glassily at Lena.

"I'm... fine... just scared! The ice... I saw how Diablo broke through. Oh, Lena, what have we done? They'll kill us if something happens to those horses!" Michelle began to sob, and Lena took her in her arms.

"I'm so glad that you didn't get hurt!" she sobbed bitterly, too, and hugged the younger girl closer. "It's all my fault! I'll tell them that you couldn't help it! I... I was such an idiot. I'm so sorry. Michelle, please forgive me!"

For a few moments, the two of them stayed intertwined, but then Lena, understanding the seriousness of their situation, wiped her eyes and in a frantic voice said, "We have to get off the lake! We have to get back – now!" Michelle understood. Scared, she nodded at the older girl and, with shaky legs, the two of them got up, hand in hand and incapable of letting go.

"What will happen if we break through?" whispered Michelle, her eyes wide with fear.

Lena swallowed hard. "We're not going to break through. Diablo weighs a lot more than we do combined. Michelle, come on, you just can't think about it. Nothing will happen, I'm sure of that."

"But what if we break through and... and go down? I don't want to die!"

"We're not going to break through! I promise!" Lena was at least as frightened as her friend, but she knew that if she gave in to this fear she wouldn't be able to take a step.

Slowly the two girls felt their way along, step by step, inch by inch, toward the safety of the shore.

Time seemed to stand still. The silence surrounding Lena and Michelle was broken only by their frightened, heavy breathing.

"I can't go on!" announced Michelle, and suddenly she stood still. "It makes me crazy to think how deep the water is under the ice!"

"Come on! Forward! The closer we get to the shore, the shallower the lake will be."

"I can't!"

"Don't be silly, Michelle! Look, it's only about ten more yards! We'll make it!" Lena said, wrapping her arms around the twelve-year-old.

"The ice is getting thinner and thinner! You can almost see the fish underneath!"

"Come on! We can't stay here!" urged Lena. However, when Michelle wouldn't move even one more yard, she lost it.

"Look, I have enough trouble! I don't want to have to explain how you froze to death once I get back to the ranch!" she screamed at Michelle, who jumped back in shock.

"I don't want to die," she repeated again in a soft voice.

"Then come on! I promise you that I'll get you safely off this lake, no matter what!" Lena didn't know where she was getting her confidence right now, but the sound of her voice was enough to get Michelle moving again.

Those were probably the longest yards of their lives, and when they finally felt firm ground under their feet they burst into tears of relief and collapsed onto the snow.

"I don't ever want to experience anything like this again," sobbed Michelle and she held on to Lena tightly.

"Me neither, believe me!"

Suddenly, Lena pushed her girlfriend away. "Do you hear what I hear?"

"What is that?"

"An engine! And the way it rattles, it can only be Carlotta's car! It's unmistakable! Do you know what that means, Michelle? They're looking for us! Come on! They have to find us!" As fast as they could on their frozen legs, the girls got up and ran.

*

"What were you two thinking?" Carlotta shouted at the shame-faced girls in her office. Lena and Michelle, wrapped in wool blankets, sat cringing in armchairs with their heads lowered, suffering Carlotta's justified rebuke in silence. "It wasn't enough that you abused my trust. No, you rode horses that didn't belong to you, and without the permission of the owners, and you put them – and yourselves – in great danger. Didn't you give any thought as to what I was going to have to tell your parents in case there was an accident?"

"I'm so sorry," Lena said. "It was all my fault! Michelle didn't want to go with me, but I told her that she would be a coward and a loser if she didn't. It wasn't her fault!"

"The fact is, she did go with you, so you both have to bear the responsibility for what happened. Sharazan and Diablo could have broken their legs! How would you ever have been able to explain that to Ricki and Kevin? Do you think a 'We're so sorry' would make that all right?"

Lena had tears in her eyes. Didn't Carlotta see that it was punishment enough for her to have to live with the idea that she had knowingly put the two most wonderful horses in the world and another person in danger?

Carlotta took a deep breath. "Lena, I don't want to see you on this ranch ever again! Do you understand me? And Michelle, I'm going to call your parents and tell them to

150

come and get you tomorrow morning. I can't have guests willfully disobeying the rules."

Lena and Michelle exchanged a painful glance. They had been so happy on this ranch, and now they themselves had managed to ruin it all and end it so quickly.

Ricki and Kevin, who stood behind Carlotta like a jury, gave each other a long look. It seemed as though they both thought the same thing.

Ricki cleared her throat awkwardly. She didn't feel comfortable. Although it had done her good at first to hear Carlotta shouting accusations at the two unfortunate girls, now she felt sorry for them, even though she could still hardly believe what the two of them had done.

"I know that I don't really have the right to say anything about this, Carlotta," she began slowly. "But in a way, I'm also a bit guilty. If I had stayed at the ranch, as I'd intended to, then none of this would have happened."

"Well, if I had thought it over, then it wouldn't have happened either," admitted Carlotta. "But you know how much responsibility I have when I take on young guests here at the ranch. If everyone just does as he or she pleases, the reputation of the ranch would be destroyed very quickly, and then I can just forget about Mercy Ranch!"

"But Michelle couldn't help it," Lena said again. "Please, Carlotta, don't send her home! It's clear that you have to throw me out, but, please, not Michelle!"

After Lena's words, only silence reigned.

Carlotta had to admit that it touched her that Lena was taking Michelle's part so strongly, and she also knew that the twelve-year-old would never have come up with an idea like going for a secret ride on her own.

"Maybe you're right," she admitted hesitantly. "Michelle can stay, but you will leave the ranch tomorrow morning! However, I will have to tell Michelle's parents what happened."

The younger girl turned pale. "Please, don't! My father would cancel riding privileges for me for the rest of my life. The horses... they're so important to me. I'd never get over it!" Michelle cried, and Lena put her arm around her to comfort her.

Carlotta sighed and rolled her eyes. If there was anything she could understand it was the desire to devote one's life to horses.

"Well, I'll think about it, considering the fact that Lena probably talked you into all this, but for now, go to your rooms! Lena, tomorrow morning, you go straight home. I'm sorry this had to happen."

"Me, too, believe me," whispered the girl, completely destroyed. With hanging heads, the two unfortunate girls, who had shamed themselves so thoroughly, slowly left the office.

After the door closed behind them, Carlotta plopped back in her armchair and rubbed her eyes tiredly.

"I think this is the first and last time I'll invite guests here to the ranch," she announced dejectedly. "I had no idea it was going to be so difficult."

"Hmm," said Ricki, still staring at the door behind which the sad Lena and Michelle had disappeared. "So, Lena really can't come back here ever again?"

Carlotta took a deep breath. "I have no choice. I have to be able to trust my helpers!"

"But don't you think that Lena has learned her lesson?"

"Of course I do! If not, then I'd really feel sorry for her!"

"And you don't want to give her another chance, maybe...

I mean here at the ranch?" Ricki asked very quietly.

Carlotta turned her chair so that she could look straight into Ricki's eyes. "Could you please tell me why you, of all people, are speaking up for her? After all, she put your horse in a lot of danger."

Ricki swallowed hard. "I don't know why, but maybe it's because I sense that she only went on this ride because she fell in love with Diablo, the way I did at the very beginning, when he still belonged to that awful Frank Cooper. And Diablo isn't seriously hurt, other than that little bit of his coat that's missing, but it'll grow back." Ricki reached for Kevin's hand.

Shaking her head, Carlotta looked at the two of them. Ricki must really have a big heart, since she seemed capable of forgiving anyone, and giving anyone a second chance, no matter what they did. Could she, Carlotta, have the same generosity?

"And it looks as if you both feel the same way, don't you?" she asked with a smile.

"All right!" she surrendered. "You did it again! As far as I'm concerned, Lena can have another chance to prove herself!"

"That's great!" Ricki beamed at Kevin. "Thanks! Can we go tell her right away?"

Carlotta laughed out loud at this, but she shook her head firmly. "No, no. Don't say anything just yet. We'll let her think about it all night. There have to be some consequences for her reckless behavior, don't you think?"

THE END